I0675902

BLOOD RUST

HOCK HOCHHEIM

WOLFPACK
PUBLISHING
— EST 2013 —

WOLFPACK
PUBLISHING
— EST 2013 —

Published in the United States by Wolfpack Publishing, Las Vegas

Wolfpack Publishing
6032 Wheat Penny Avenue
Las Vegas, NV 89122

wolfpackpublishing.com

Paperback ISBN 978-1-64734-046-9
eBook ISBN 978-1-64734-045-2

BLOOD RUST

CHAPTER 1
ALPHONSO THE CREPE HANGER

Tonight I met Al. Was I crazy to meet him alone? A.K.A. Alphonso the Crepe hanger. Al Pauelka was with the guy who shot me in the stomach eight years ago. Al was an accomplice. His pizon, his goomba - Louis Geampalova, "Louie" shot me in the gut, and then shot me right in the head when I bent over from the one in the gut. Louie got life, you know, because I lived. But he still got life because he shot a cop. Al tried to shoot me too, but Al missed, and all my lousy shots back at them missed, and only ran them off.

NYPD caught them within two weeks. Jailed them. But Al worked a deal with the Feds and did only eight years. Today, this very afternoon, he was freed. Did Al mean to finish the hit tonight? Was I crazy to meet him again? Here? Alone? At night, under the George Washington Bridge? On the Jersey side?

Fact is? I am crazy. So what? So the men in the white smocks tell me. Fact is, that 9mm bullet in my gut didn't kill me. Not the one in my head either. Not fast, anyway.

Just slow. Like a slow-motion bullet. They took the bullets out with stainless steel pliers at the hospital, but they are still killing me like they are still in me. They killed off a lot in me. I ain't that cop no more. And I ain't that daddy of two girls no more. Ain't that husband. Ain't that son. Ain't that Mister-Mister. That person did die off, from the slow, slow lead poisoning. What's left here? Just slow poison. Forty-five caliber arsenic. Just a meat puppet moving forward. Who is pulling my strings? Nobody knows. I don't.

Sometimes I forget I was shot in the head. Sounds crazy, huh? But I told you I was crazy. It slips my mind if you can imagine, like a glass jar slides off a table. Skip. Slip. Oops. I remember I was shot in the stomach because, well, I can see my stomach. I can look at the scar, but I can't see my head. See my brain. See into my brain. Wrong side of my eyeballs. So I forget sometimes.

So, it was night. It was cold on the lot of Ross Dock picnic grounds. Sea level. Palisades Interstate Park. I wandered over to the water's edge. The Hudson River lapped around the rocks and stones. It stunk like dead fish and dead birds. Not dead people. I know that smell. The difference between hot dogs and hamburgers. Between cherry pie and apple pie. New dead. Old dead. Even wet dead, dry dead. When you were a street cop, and detective in homicide and organized crime, the fragments of death cling to your nose hairs.

The water made its murky, slop sounds. A hundred feet away the grey water cut around the giant, bridge stanchion. The cars on the GW Bridge way above just rocked on in their double-decker heavens. Over the river, New York City and its traffic lights blurred from a very thin fog. I could almost make out the top of Grant's Tomb. It was almost my tomb. That's where Louie shot me down, where Al tried to and watched. Right on the steps of Grant's

Tomb. That was my Ground Zero. My 9-11. I faded out of that one. I faded back in a different color. A different skin. Out with the old. In with the new.

I could see the whole skyline at sea level, this fucking city I detest. The city that shot me and stomped me and killed me. Al Pavelka was just a haunted finger of a gangrene city that stuck his unclean, dirty nail into me. My own fingers tightened and squeezed around the snub-nosed revolver in my pants pocket, inside the baggy pants I got from Goodwill last week. They were nice pants. Tan. I got a belt for 70 cents. With my free hand, I pulled the leather jacket I shoplifted from Target tighter around me as the smelly chill ballooned in. The gun? I stole it from a house in Paramus. Yeah, I burgle. I steal. And that shit ain't the half of it.

The river mist hung on my eyebrows. I looked up at the granite cliffs they call the Palisades of Jersey. If all life begins in New York City and runs outward, then life has to climb the Palisade Cliffs. On this Jersey side of the bridge, just south of me there once were rotted docks and the rough jerks who worked them and the smelly bars they went to. Now the shoreline is full of condos and new stores all the way down to the Lincoln Tunnel.

Okay. Okay. Where is the wop mook? Eleven days ago, Al Pavelka called me from upstate, from the Fishkill Correctional Facility.

He said, "Rusty, this is Al Pavelka."

"How the fuck did you get this phone number?"

"I got to ta tawk wit you."

"HOW THE FUCK did you get my phone number?"

"In person. In person. We need to tawk. You know it's important because I am calling you. In eleven days. I get paroled. Meet me at 9 p.m., on the 27th, under the GW Bridge. Jersey-side. Ross Dock Park. We need to tawk. Rusty. It's important."

"Important to who…?" and the creep hung up on me.

Now, the last thing I care to do is haul my greasy ass out, in a stolen car, mind you, at night, mind you, to meet some Mafia trigger man, mind you, - who tried to kill me eight years ago, and he wants to tell me…what? He found a plastic statue of Jesus in the corner of a jail cell? And it glowed? What? He's sorry? Sorry! Or some such shit? Easing his conscious means nothing to me and my conscious. My conscious is on the steps of Grant's Tomb over there. I could seriously just shoot and kill Al. Seriously. Depends on if he comes alone.

And anyway, how'd that fuck get my phone number? My new Wal-Mart telephone number? I change phones about every month to deal drugs and not get tracked, you know, if I can remember to change phones. About every month.

After they scraped me off the stone steps of Grant's Tomb and they tried to reconstruct my deconstruct, and the so-called authorities started bracing Al. Al started talking. And, as a result, Al starts walking. Al cut a deal for intelligence info on rival gangs, not his own gang, mind you. He's still good and tight with his homies, shaving down the competition for his home team. He blazed a path for the Feds, but he kept his own family enterprise clean and intact. I know. I've been there. I'll talk to rats to sink a ship, even when the rat's ship stays afloat. They charged Al with attempted murder, and then they wheeled and dealed into a rollover. Al took a short stint. I took two slugs. They took 7 inches of my intestine. They took an inch or so of my brain goop. And Al? Al got out this afternoon. I oughta kill him. If I really cared, I should shoot him dead on sight. Cared is a tricky word though, you know? Sometimes I feel a little distant from it all, you know? Whatever. Distant. Mystical. Detached. Yeah, detached is the best word. Like my former body parts.

But since he called me that night? I know one thing. I haven't used much crystal meth. Not much dope. Since that phone call, I am so pissed, or jazzed, or what? I started thinking about the call day and night. Thinking about it hard. Al. Can't sleep. Al. What could Al want to tell me? Al. If we meet, is he going to kill me? Al. Finish the job and collect on an old contract? The Mob is like that. The Five Apes, too. Al. The Mob don't like no unfinished business. Neither do the Five Apes. Only way to know, is to go. To come here, tonight. Then I will know. Then, if I die, I will kill the bastard too with this small, rat-killer pistol in my pocket.

I spat on the gravel. The spit looked like it had a little blood in it. So what? I got holes in me. Got shit eaten on me. Got foam that comes out my mouth. Sometimes it's got a little red in it. So what?

You know I didn't even testify in my own attempted murder hearings? I couldn't testify. Wounded badly. I made an appearance in court strapped into a wheelchair. The newspapers covered the story big time. Front page Daily News. Front page, New York Post. Cop in a wheelchair. They wheeled me in, and I just sat there, listening like a crippled stump. I think the pictures showed my head all bandaged up. I remember the pictures. I was shot in the stomach? Wait now, was I shot in the head, too? Wait now… anyway, I couldn't even talk back then. Just moaned like a zombie. Slobbered. A little red in the slobber down my jaw.

It is the sweet, sweet poetry of the crusty, crusty street to meet with your hit man when he calls you to tell you something important. Ain't it? A dead reckoning of all reckonings. And therefore, henceforth, I await. With an itchy finger inside the trigger guard, I anxiously await the rat bastard with my rat killer gun.

CHAPTER 2
MANNEQUINS

At 9:55, a midsize Jap car, newer model, turned down the park drive. Jap or Yugoslavian, who knows? New York plates. I notice shit like that. Old habit. It crunched slowly across the gravel parking lot. I stood ten feet from my little stolen sedan and waited. The gun in my hand, hand in my pocket. Heart in my mouth. Red spit on my tongue. Killing in my mind. Rat bastard.

The car stopped far off. Two men inside. The passenger opened his door, and Al Pavelka himself stepped out. Al wore a long overcoat. Bare hands. Empty hands. Beard and long hair. The driver remained a gray statue, a distracting shape behind the wheel. I could at least see his fleshy white paws on the steering wheel. No gloves. Good. Killers like to wear gloves. Al wasn't wearing gloves either. I, on the other hand, had my gloves on.

"Rusty," Al said, "I come here to..."

"How'd you get my phone number?"

He showed me the palms of his empty, pale white hands,

and I thought about shooting both of them anyway. Shoot the hands down at the heels. Putting bullets into his heels and driving lead into his wrists and up the forearms and into his elbows. Oh, that would hurt. Wouldn't it?

"Rusty, do you remember Steverino Downing?" Pavelka asked me. "You pinched him for murder back in 04? The China Doll case?"

"Steverino. Yeah." I said. The China Doll? Holy fuck, 2004? I can remember that?

Al worked himself closer. He got halfway to me.

"His son was in jail with me upstate. I got to know this kid real good. Rusty, Steverino was set up. Steverino did not kill the China Doll, Rusty. You were played. Set up. Steverino will get the needle in a month and half, and he is fucking innocent. He didn't kill nobody."

"And you are telling me this because?"

"Because he's innocent, and you been played. I believe his son. Either way, that should piss you off. I know you. Being played, sending a man to death row should piss you off. You were a good detective…"

Detective. What a…what a distant word. He might as well a said circus clown. Or NASCAR driver. Like…like who? What?

"I am not a detective anymore."

"I know you…"

"No, you don't know me. You know somebody else. You guys shot somebody else. You do not know me. I am the skid row bum that's left. The shadow."

"But it should still piss you off, Rusty. Hey, I could get into trouble for telling you this, but you were played. Look, I am close to the kid. I'm doing this for the kid. I promised the kid I would tell you this. Maybe you'll do something about the set up and maybe save this Downing guy. Save his life and shit."

"Hmmm," I growled. "Save his life. Who's in the car?"

"Just a friend. Just a ride. I got out this afternoon, Rusty. We drove straight here. I did some hard years for your shooting, Rusty. I have paid my debts. The guards would beat me whenever they could catch me between cameras because I was in on a cop shooting."

Debts? I just stared at him. Coulda, woulda, shoulda shot him in the forehead right there. Dead would be better than what I am. They shot me in the stomach, and the bullet went out my lower back. The bullet snagged my soul and it flew away like a transparent kite high over Grant's Tomb. My soul, like a spider web in the wind. I can't find that ghost of me anymore. And he says debts, he says? Paid? To who?

"I did not shoot you, Rusty, Louie did."

I walked forward slowly.

"Don't even go there," I said.

"I…"

"I suppose you are gonna go see Tony the Stake, Louis Puntinni and the gang and have a big pizza party with hookers tonight?"

"Nope. No, I'm not. A lot's changed in these years, Rusty."

"When you get to the party Al, will they all call you your old nickname? Alphonso the Crepe hanger?"

"No party, Rusty."

"Hmmm."

"I'm sorry, Rusty."

We stared at each other. Al shook his head side to side. You know, like in frustration. The driver turned the steering wheel and the tires crunched across the gravel. Al caught the exit signal.

"Well, I'm going home. I just wanted to tell you about Downing."

He stepped forward with an outstretched hand, as if I might shake it. I looked at his empty hand. It looked like an on and off switch. One that I could throw.

"They tell me Al, I have impulse problems. They tell me I want instant gratification. They tell me that people in this world are like store dummies to me. Mannequins. This is what the doctors tell me. I got a .38 in my right hand, Al, if the hand comes outta' this pocket, a gun comes out with it. It won't be to shake your fucking hand. I will shoot you dead."

Al stopped, grimaced and dropped his hand. His little beady eyes looked sad to me. Awww.

He turned for the open car door. "Steverino did not kill the China Doll, Rusty. Think about it. It was Apes. The Five Apes. It was the Mob. China was in on it, too."

"China," I repeated. "Hey!" I said.

He looked back at me.

"How'd you get my fucking phone number?"

"Rusty? You and me? We are now in the same business. We are in the same phone book."

He sat down in the car and shut the door. I watched it drive off the lot. It turned up the road and climbed the Palisade Cliffs. Gone. Gone like a dream. Did that really even happen? Because, you know? Sometimes I see shit. See people. I don't trust that they are there.

The "same business," he said to me. And that business is crime. I am in the crime business now. I stood there in the cold Hudson mist. I stood at the calloused feet of the giant city for ten minutes? I don't know. The petrified legs of the George Washington bridge sticking out over my head. I don't know how long. Maybe more than ten minutes? I can lose track of time, too. I do that. I kind of stare sometimes, and I get a tight feeling in my jaw and a feeling of, like a, bad juice comes in my mouth. Sometimes it's a rusty red. You ever have that? One time 30 minutes passed like it was a minute.

The mist increased, and I wiped it off my face. I should a shot Alphonso the Crepe Hanger. But, then his driver would have shot me? Me, him, too?

Steverino Downing? I stood there thinking about it in my funk stupor. I'd collared Downing back in my true-blue days when I was with the NYPD Homicide. I arrested him for the murder of a Chinese diplomat's wife in Manhattan. The rag papers and the Times called it the China Doll Murder. Sounds wicked. Sells like any good scandal. The Chinese woman was beautiful. She was a treasure. Smart. Gorgeous. Poised. Posh. Jet black hair like a thick silk like you've never seen. A treasure. Red lips. She was a real China Doll. And, she was the wife of a Chinese diplomat that worked at the embassy. That, alone, made it all full of international intrigue. We didn't see it that. I…I didn't see it that way. It was just a murder, rape and abduction. No intrigue. No international intrigue.

Let me see. How? How, did I make that case? Oh yeah. The case was made by an ID! A simple identification. A next-door neighbor fingered Downing leaving the scene with the body wrapped in a rug or something. Stupid fuck Downing hauled the corpse to Connecticut, the only state in New England with the death penalty and buried said Oriental remains, carpet and all, in the woods. How did we…oh yeah, a tipster phoned in, called Crime Stoppers saying he saw a man burying something that looked like a body up there in the Connecticut woods. Got his license plate. We found the body. Cadaver dogs. We filed the murder case up there in the death penalty state. It was the usual option. More blood for the buck.

A tugboat horn hit a deep, mellow octave, and the bellow rattled through my lungs and woke me up from my fog in a fog. I get like this, did I tell you? It is like a coma. A smoky mess of thoughts gets in my brain. I keep thinking I will get to the bottom of something, but I get, like, hypnotized, and I get to the bottom of nothing! I can't get to the bottom of thoughts, but I keep digging down at the smoke.

I walked back, slipped into my stolen Buick sedan and got the holy hell out of there. Who the hell cares about Steverino Downing and the Chinese Doll? Driving the road up the Palisade Cliffs, I started thinking about that neighbor who saw Downing. Said he saw Downing carrying out a big, rolled carpet, bent at his shoulder. He put it in his car. And he drove out the driveway. What was his name? If Downing was really fingered, then this witness lied, and the tipster who called in the body site in Connecticut lied, too. Why'd they do that?

But why should I care, anyway? I ain't all that anymore. I have meth to peddle in Journal Square in Jersey City. I got whores to run. I'm in the business of crime, like Alphonso said. Hey, I'm in the book! The crime book. The underworld registry. I've got mannequins to ruin. I got... what was that guy's name?

Steverino. Al Pavelka. Grant's Tomb. China Doll. The Five Apes. The names scraped through my brain like a sandpaper tornado. Mannequins! A bunch of mannequins. My throat tightened up. Al Pavelka, Grant's Tomb, China Doll, Five Apes, Steverino. Rotate. Rotate. Rotate. Grant's...

CHAPTER 3
WORMS RUNNING FREE

I am not sure I am a psychopath or not. What do they call it now? A sociopath? The politically correct psychopath is a sociopath. I just don't know what "path" I am on. I mean, I know what that is, I just don't know if I fit the diagnosis. I woke up that morning with paths on my mind, so I quickly tried to doze off again.

Bang on my foot! What?

"Hey!" I heard. A cop kicked my foot again. That's how I woke up. Cop kicking my foot. My head snapped down, and I looked at him. I rubbed my neck. It is hard on the neck sleeping while sitting up on a park bench. Head all hanging back like a broke doll.

"Hey, you see anybody near that car, over there? The Buick?"

"Huh? What?" I asked. A Fort Lee city cop was standing over me. I squinted from the morning sun.

"That Buick over there. You see anybody around it?" he repeated.

"No, officer?"

Well, just me. My stolen Buick.

A tow truck was pulling my ride from the diagonal parking space!

"How long you been here?" he asked.

"Oh, an hour? Took a walk. Sat here to read the paper." I tapped the newspaper on my lap. "Must have…dozed off."

He looked at the Hudson Dispatch on my knee. Then, he looked at my eyes.

"Okay, good day, sir." He walked over to the tow truck.

Street thug rules. Never sleep in a stolen car. Unless you're in Antarctica and just have, too. Always wear driving gloves. That's why God invented them. No prints.

I stood up and stretched, folded the paper under my arm and walked slowly south on West Side Drive – the road atop the Palisade Cliffs that overlooks the NYC skyline. Even though it was, like, I don't know, what? A 35-plus mile walk to Jersey City, minus my ride.

After I left the park the night before, I felt this…this suffocating dread come over me. My stomach felt like it was trying to digest a large slate stone. Then, I got real, real doghouse tired. It was only midnight! I got as far as Fort Lee, parked the stolen heap, pulled a newspaper from a trash can and sat on a bench under some trees, off the dark sidewalk by a park. Bedtime. The paper is just something I was supposed to be reading if I fell asleep and people saw me in the morning. The paper worked all the time and did once again for the Ft. Lee flatfoot.

I walked on and on. I was a flatfoot once in Manhattan and the Bronx. Back then I was in a squad car. Then I got my gold shield as a detective. Worked all kinds of crime. Homicide, too. That's when I worked dozens of murders, and the China Doll was one of them. Then I grinded on to the Organized Crime Squad. All told, 22 years of grinding.

But, I, too, was a flatfoot once, tapping bums' feet with a nightstick. Right over there to my left. Right over the Hudson River. Now I take care of my business in Jersey. It's personal business. Personally destroying people's lives business, one day at a time.

I kept walking. Hey! I still had my gun in my pocket! If that cop frisked, me he would have tapped it. I don't know what I would have done, but it would have been quick and bad, because I have no time to waste. I lost my own time. I am on somebody else's time that ain't my time no more. Could I shoot a cop? I have never had to, even though cops tried to shoot me, even when I was a cop. The Five Apes. Wait. Is that right? Did I get that right? Cops tried to shoot me when I was a cop? Oh yeah, the Five…Apes? Apes over there. Over there in New York City on my bad side, my left side.

Still had that new ID in my pocket. If that cop had asked me for ID, I would have handed him my Victor Penski driver's license. I killed Victor in a rest stop in Maine two years ago. He was a happy-go-lucky guy, divorced and moving to Canada to start a new life. I helped him, really. New lives are hard. And Canada? Come on! I didn't kill Victor to save him, though, I killed Victor because he looked a little bit like me. Around the edges, you know? I didn't kill him right away. I kidnapped him first and made him drive off into the woods. Made him walk off into the woods. Killed him and buried him. You don't want to know how I killed him because I didn't have any weapons with me. I improvised. Buried him good. Deep. His car was full of boxes of his shit. I went through his stuff and took what I needed. Burned the rest. Eventually I pushed his car off a cliff into a rock quarry into a deep-water pit where I know mobsters push cars and guys into out in West Jersey. It's a secret place we all know about where we drop people and can trust they stay dropped. I used Victor's credit cards for a while, early on, but it was too perfect to last forever. It will never be that easy a kill again, you know, kill a guy who looked like me, who was trying to start over in a new country? Wow, what a lucky break. It was perfect. I guess everyone still thinks Victor is in Canada living a lost, hippy life with the Eskimos. "Nanook" Victor of the North.

Victor's driver license expires next year and I am going to have to kill someone else, I guess. He will be my third for ID. Nothing personal. I just need some ID, you know? That's all. They have to look like me. You know, he has to be about 6 foot tall. Medium build. He has to have reddish hair, be about 45 years old and look a little Irish. And I ain't pretty. I noticed in a McDonalds' bathroom mirror the other day I look really different. I don't look like me anymore. My face. That face is a mask anyway, so what? That gray thing of flesh hanging on my face bones just needs to look like a picture on a real driver's license of some other meat puppet's face meat.

I took a breather from my walk to Journal Square and leaned on the thick, blue stone wall. There she was. Manhattan. Whereabouts would East 76th Street be? That street is where the China Doll was murdered. I guess it would be right about…there. No…there! What was the name of the witness neighbor? If Steverino Downing didn't rape and kill this doll, who did rape and shoot her, and why would a neighbor lie to me about it? Why would someone else frame a guy from Harlem named Steverino? How could they be connected to a witness in Connecticut for such a frame-up?

"Hey buddy?" A shabby man said to my left. "You got a buck for a hungry Joe?"

"You got a death wish?" I answered.

He sneered at me and walked on. I needed a buck from him!

There was no DNA to speak of back then. A rape kit done up in Connecticut. We guessed he used a condom but the rape injuries were there. No magic science. That was all just half-assed, science fiction back then. There was no big money to run new and expensive DNA tests on every case back then anyway. Certainly not open and shut cases that lying neighbors set in stone for you. Was there possible DNA left in the NYPD evidence room? People in the pen get vindicated every day from cases that are decades old. What about this Steverino guy? People get cleared all the time that are on Death Row, like by the Freedom Foundation.

I suddenly brewed a flaming ball of bile in my gut and thought I would upchuck over the wall. Then…whew…I got real tired. Dizzy kind of tired. Like I just shot-up some bad horse. I looked at a park bench on the boulevard. Oh boy, I needed to be on that thing. The clear day got fuzzy and small in my eyes. That green bubble made it up to my mouth, and I belched it out. Wretched and relieved all at the same time.

If I fell asleep on the bench, would I wake up wondering if I was a sociopath again? Do psychopaths wonder if they are psychopaths? Can they care that deeply? Do they? Does Steverino Downing wonder what the fuck happened to him? Does Victor Penski wonder what happened to him? I needed a drink and a big pill of something. Al said Steverino will be dead in a month or so, and maybe he and Victor Penski can talk about it all on a park bench in their next fairytale land.

Meanwhile, I slowly headed for the park bench. The sun felt so warm. But, next, you know what? I saw Steverino sitting right on that park bench, a much older Steverino though than I remember. My head twisted back. His afro was gray. His bottom lip turned down like he'd had a stroke. He was arguing with a corpse, a gray, eaten-out, worm-ridden, dead guy in a suit, with a hole in his head. Well, my jaw dropped. I circled the bench like I was stalking a deer. The dead guy was Victor! And I was just thinking about him! About them! The both of them! He just sat there, staring ahead. Eyes all bugged out. I couldn't understand what Steverino was saying to him. Then the worms on Victor's face changed it all around, like a sculptor moving clay in animation. The worms pushed, and moved the meat on his face. When they were done with shoving it around? It was my face! My dead face! Me. Me looking right at me, only I looked like Dracula or something. Me, sitting on that bench, and Steverino was yelling at me. Wait, wait! He wasn't yelling! He was singing to me.

"And the masters make the rules,
for the wise men,
and the fools."

What the hell? He was singing to him. To me. To us. Over and over. I just stood there on the sidewalk, mesmerized. Then, I swear I felt those worms crawling around my own head. On my face. In my mouth. I started to gag.

"Get a grip," I mumbled. "This ain't real. This can't be real!" But I couldn't get a grip. My corpse on the bench looked at me and said, "Get a grip, doofus."

He smiled at me. Some of our yellow teeth fell out. I started to gag and cry. I grabbed a handful of revolver in my pocket and shot my corpse right in the throat. I killed myself. A burst of gray throat dust filed the air. That bullet shook my eardrums, and I fell back on the grass. On my back! I peed my pants. But, when I looked up again? The park bench was suddenly empty. Empty! They both were gone. There was a splintered, bullet hole in the wooden back of the empty bench. A dead me was once there. Now gone.

"Holy…fuck," I mumbled. "I am losing my fucking mind, here. I killed my own dead self." And I me, and Victor…he is me now. I stood up and looked around. It was about 10:30 a.m. and, so far, no one was around the Palisades or Hudson County Park on this weekday morning to see or hear this pistol shot crack. Never a flatfoot around when you need one. I got to go.

As sick as I felt, I walked, and briskly I might add, away from this noisy mess. My wet pants clung to my leg which sucked because, you know, it's pee. My pee, but it's pee. I saw myself in the reflections of parked car windows in glimpses like flash cards. I knew I was shuffling along, coat collar up, mumbling, like a paranoid, crack-addict freak, Aqualung, homeless person. Was I just another paranoid, crack freak? Am I homeless?

I was still crying, but not for anyone. Not for myself. Just releasing, like I peed. I peed, and I cried. And I peed, and I cried. Just a loss of water, that's all. I don't know why. Maybe something in me is crying somewhere. I do have holes in me. Like some sad cell in there? Or a homesick amoeba? I just ain't attached to the crying spot anymore to know.

Some of those graveyard worms squirmed on the sidewalk ahead of me. Just a few of them. I leaped and landed right on them to squish them good. I know I looked like a hopscotch, retard, but, hey! I saw what those worms could do. They mustn't be allowed to run free. What was the name of that neighbor that fingered Steverino Downing? I asked myself. The worm what fingered Steverino Downing for murder? Manhattan glittered off to my left, and I got to go over there and find out, though some of the cops over there will kill me on sight if they see me. The Five Apes. Even my old best friend might kill me on sight. But I got to see him. But why, again?

CHAPTER 4
ABERRANT EYEBALLS

I pounded and pounded on the tenement door. The hallway smelled like 16 different countries worth of food, mixed with a dead rat and wet rug.

"Sheneequa, let me in, it's RUSTY!"

Latches. Chains. The door cracked open, and I saw Sheneequa's, big brown, left eyeball.

"What do you want? It is two in the morning," she whispered with a raspy tone that told me she was angry.

"Shen, I need in. Look. I need a shower."

We both heard a door creak open down the hall and looked. A black male peeked out and said, "Let that noisy muther fucker in, girl!"

More latches and chains. Shen swung open the door. I marched in. The apartment was dark. One of her kids slept on the couch.

Shen was naked. She stood in front of me, crossed her arms and swung her hip to the left.

"What the fuck you want?" she asked.

"I just walked here all the way from Fort Lee."

"So?"

"So, I need to rest."

"Oh, you need a rest."

"Just a little. Look, let me lay down here on the floor. You go back to bed and in the morning…"

"I got three kids to get off to school, and myself…in my morning. What's your morning?"

"What the fuck you want?" a man said.

"Hi, Hershel," I said to the naked black man in the bedroom doorway.

"Oh, oh, hi Rusty," he answered. His tone lowered, respectfully when he realized who I was.

Hershel knows, if I jumped all kind a crazy, I would gut his ass in a minute. I would take his place in Sheneequa's bed in a second and make him sleep naked on the fire escape. You see, Hershel is a good man who lives by the rules. Me, Rusty. Rusty is a bad man. I make the rules. Minute-by-minute. And some rules, I admit, are flat, stellar, fire escape crazy.

Sheneequa knows me for years. Shen's drug years. Shit, one of her lighter-skinned kids may even be mine. I don't know. Don't really care. I do let her fuck with me a little. Get sassy. Throw that hip out. Get feisty. I like her sassy, but not too much. I have punched her lights out. And I will do it again.

I lay down on the living room floor under the window. I rolled my Goodwill jacket up for a pillow. Hershel touched Sheneequa's elbow, then caught it between his thumb and forefinger. He pulled her back into the bedroom and shut the door.

I stared at the cracked ceiling. The carpet smelled like dead man, dirty feet and cat shit. Darnell, Sheneequa's 9-year-old was sound asleep on the couch. I'd walked all those miles today. All the way from Fort Lee, hugging the

Hudson River, hugging that view of New York. I wanted to. It was some kind of super-freak, hypnotized walk. Zoned out on the Chinese lady. The China Doll.

There, in the quiet, I heard the muffled TVs and talk of tenement life. The occasional shriek. The wild, cackling laugh. The coughing fit. Cop cars and ambulance sirens passed by on the street below. Then I passed out cold. I dreamed of tall men in suits and overcoats looming over me, mumbling. They wore fedoras like the old FBI guys. They looked like the stone faces on Easter Island. They were assessing me for something.

They said in order, "A bear."

"A bear rants."

"Aberrant. Aberrant behavior."

They nodded their long grey heads at each other in stony agreement.

When I opened my aberrant eyes, Darnell stood right over me, little, skinny rug rat that he was, in nothing but a pair of white underwear.

"Hi, Uncle Rusty."

"Hi, Darnell."

Sheneequa burst from the bedroom hall and, in a whirlwind, whisked her teenage son, Damon, her daughter, Laquisha and then Darnell into a ready-for-school tornado. I've seen this before. Hershel, dressed in the brown uniform of some loser company walked through the living room, kissed Sheneequa on the cheek like it was some badge of courage for him to do that in front of me. He looked at me. I raised my eyebrows.

"Whatever," I said lowly. "Hey, don't forget your lunch box, faggot!"

He left.

"That is some man you got there, Shen," I said to her. I snatched a piece of toast from Darnell's plate. "And you are some woman to work him up to be such a mighty man."

Shen sneered at me. Within minutes the whole crew poured out the front door. She was last. And, it was speech time.

"When you leave? You leave with nothing. You lock this door and pull it to."

"You're a good ol' friend, Shen."

"All your old friends are dead, in the pen, or in rehab," she said. "You ain't got no old friends, old man. All your new friends are drug addicts." She pointed to the door-knob. Then she pushed the automatic lock button on the knob, and slammed the heavy door shut and left.

I ate like a pig. I took a shower and shaved and raided her teenage son's room. Damon was a huge kid, an athlete and, in his closet, he had white shirts, a sports coat and khaki pants. All waiting for me? For me! He even folded some clean socks and had shiny shoes just a bit too big for me. But I laced them tight and spread my toes inside them. Nice.

I piled up my peed pants, Goodwill jacket, shirt and shit and wrote a note on a piece of paper, "Wash this." I piled it all in the middle of the dining table, so they wouldn't be missed.

Then I looked for money. I raided the kid's change jars and tossed Shen's bedroom. Damned if the bitch didn't buy a fucking safe! It was small. I could carry it out, but to do what? Crack it? Cut it? No tools. No time. For a minute I wished I could lock up my pistol in there and keep it from Darnell. I can't take it where I am going today. I shoved the pistol deep under Shen's mattress between it and the box spring. I thought about leaving it cocked and pointed at Hershel's side...a little bump and BANG! But maybe one of the kids might jump on the bed?

Not much geetus from this place. I walked out and did push the lock button on the knob as Massa Mama ordered me to do. I don't want nobody stealing my peed-pants. I pulled the door closed and left the Pelton Arms Tenement projects like a new man. All up in a suit. Squeaky new shoes. At least on the outside, I was new stuff.

I was headed to the bus stop to catch the bus to the Port Authority, New York, New York. From there, on to One Police Plaza, to see an old…friend. Maybe Shen is right. Maybe, I don't have any old friends anymore. Just enemies and drug addicts. The Five Apes.

I stroked my smooth cheek. I didn't need that shave too badly. I keep up with that. You see - a criminal, a real player - needs to stay clean-shaven. It's all psychological when dealing with the cops. If your clothes are clean and your hair is clean and short, and your face is clean-shaven? The little-peanuts-for-cop-brains think that you are respectable. If you wear a tie? You are a republican touring from the Capital. If you dress in gangsta, hip hop or just plain stank? With a goofy ass, new giant, ball cap with a flat bill, all cocked to one side and a pair of pants so low it's like they were hanging on your dick like a hook? They are gonna' spend time with you. Cops will spend time with you. Bad time. Asking fool questions, and that is not the kind of time I want to spend with police officers. I like my time with police officers to be shorter than a simultaneous wave and a smile. One wave that means hello and goodbye at the same time. Not much chance of that today, though. Did I tell you I was a cop once? Did I tell you I was bound for One Police Plaza? The 1PP. The Puzzle Palace.

I stood one block away from the bus stop and waited. My bus passed me, but it wasn't time yet. Old ladies passed me, but it wasn't time yet.

I waited.

I waited.

I waited.

Then the next bus was coming…coming…coming…and an old lady was coming…coming…coming. She walked past me. Okay! And the bus was about half a block away now.

I charged. I hit her with a body block from behind, like a football player, and I grabbed that big juicy purse right off her shoulder. She went flying, and I went flying. She flew face first into the brick wall of a building, and I flew off for the bus stop. You can't have her standing and screaming! You have to have her stunned and down below the average line of sight. Lower than parked cars, that is. Just do the math! The bus made its stop. People were getting on, and I climbed aboard as the last person. The bus driver, my unwitting getaway accomplice, yanked his door handle and the metal door hit me in the rear. Since I was holding a purse, I made a little surprise sound and a giggle like I was a man/woman vesty who liked big purses.

I stood on the inside bus steps, opened the purse and scrounged through it. The driver, a fat white man glared down at me, grimaced and then gassed the bus into traffic.

I said in my best prissy, queery voice. Super lisp, "Oh, now, let me sssseee, now."

I found a change purse, zipped it open and dropped the coins in his rattling, glass coin catcher. It chugged the change. I walked to the rear of the bus and took a back-row seat. It was a hobo Christmas as I fingered through the purse for booty. $60 in twenties! I could get to the police headquarters and back, maybe even get a lunch and a fresh newspaper as a walk-around prop. I found a prescription bottle. Mrs. Lillian Lipshitz. I read the contents, "take as needed for pain." I emptied the pills out and shoved them into my coat pocket as we entered into the Holland Tunnel to NYC. I expected pain this day. Real pain and lots of it.

I rested my forehead on the warm bus window and rode out the pothole bumps. Sometimes these bangs hurt a little. I like that. I like guessing when the pain would come. Then I sat back in the flat cushioned seat and stared at the oily spot on the window glass that my head left behind. Wrinkled like a fingerprint. I spotted one of my red hairs stuck in the oil. Was that all there was to be left of me in this world? A small, oily stain with a strand of hair? A hair freed from my scalp, this fucked-up body. From me. Lucky hair.

My wife use to cut my hair with clippers in the dining room, you know. My kids loved it. They loved to try to catch the hair as it fell off. They giggled and collected it up from the wood floor in the dining room I refinished and saved it. I wonder if they still have my hair somewhere? Like in a box? Stuck in a book? Like you save dead relatives' hair? What were their names again? What were my kid's names again?

Mrs. Lipshitz had no pills for all my stains. The stain that my head creates each day I open my aberrant eyeballs and press them against the world.

CHAPTER 5
CATS EAT RATS

I walked into the party, like I was walking onto a yacht, minus the apricot scarf. I am so vain, I thought that all eyes were upon me. I am so vain. Five Apes' eyes. I thought all the eyeballs and cameras of Police Plaza One were aimed right on me. Guess what, Carly? They were on me.

Did I mention I hadn't been in this building in about 13 years? Not much had changed. Maybe the air conditioning was better. The same statue of a cop in uniform with a boy. They have some 911 commemoratives on the walls. I missed all that stuff. I slept through 9-11 on a heroin buzz in Atlantic City. I woke up, and there was a big space in the New York City sky. Whatever.

I approached a woman at the marble kiosk.

"Captain Richard Powell Dickerson, please," I said with a winning smile.

"May I say who is asking?"

"You may certainly. Tell him it's his old partner, Rusty, here to see him."

Her eyebrow rose. I raised my opposite eyebrow.

She got busy on the phone. But not fast enough. In just a minute I spotted two large, plainclothes men marching my way. Their faces were…unhappy. They saw me. I may be vain? But this was really about me. All about me.

"Cranston and Macelroy," I said with my own unhappy face. Now there were three unhappy faces in the Plaza lobby.

Each one grabbed an arm, and they carted me through the lobby and into the exit lane right beside the metal detectors where employees walk, and up a hallway. Damn! I could have carried that snub-nosed in after all with this kind of airborne, diplomatic escort. The guards did not stop us. They just watched us go by. Damon's shoes barely touched the floor.

"Good to see you boys still upholding the law," I said.

Cranston threw open an office door, and they tossed me inside. They barged into the room right behind me.

"Get out!" Cranston roared to two women sitting at desks. Frightened, these two chicks jumped up, yelped and teeter-tottered past us in their spike high heels. Why do men like women in high heels? What is it exactly that…

"Hey!" Mac hit me in the face twice. He had such small fists though they didn't do much. The old expression of "grin and bear it" holds true when taking a few to the face. Grit your teeth in a grin, and don't let your head bounce too much, you…WHOA! Be like a movie stuntman, and go with the flow, just ahead of the flow, actually. Then Cranston hit me a good one. I flowed right over a desk. Everything on it went with me. I hit the floor, and I enjoyed the momentary respite of being on one side of the desk and them on the other. Did I saw momentary? I mean seconds. They both crashed into me again.

"You gotta' lotta'nerve comin' here, Rusty!" Mac growled, pummeling my torso and face while Cranston jumped me from behind and held my arms. With each swing, Mac's sport jacket flew open, and I could see his police badge on his belt. And his pistol. I started to laugh until a knee landed in my groin.

He must have gotten tired of pelting me. Pelting is an exhausting business, as I have been on the pelter end of this myself a time or two. When he stopped, and Cranston let go of me, I thought I would say or do something cool. I opened my mouth but, you know, I fell straight down to my knees instead. Limp. Damn body…hello! Get back with me! Surprised, I landed face first on the carpet. Staying still meant getting kicked, so I crawled off like a drooling, groaning sloth, grabbed onto a chair and climbed up to my feet. I sneezed blood. My nose was fucked up good. I must have looked like the insides of a car wreck.

"What did you expect, coming in here?" Cranston asked.

"A lot more than that," I said. I spit some blood. "I had sex with a 90-pound hooker last night that hit me harder than that with her pussy," I spit more blood and chuckled at my situation. Before they could say or do something else, I slowly lifted an evil, evil eye at them. Then, from behind my back, I lifted Cranston's pistol in my right hand. You see, when douchbag boy held me? My right hand went a fishing. I went fishing for his gun, and I hooked it.

The two dicks stood there, astonished. Cranston slapped at his hip and must have felt that empty holster collapse under his jacket. The gun was a small Glock 9mm. Their faces changed like time-lapse, rotting pumpkins.

"You gonna' shoot us right here in the police headquarters, Rusty?" Pumpkin One asked. But it wasn't really a question.

"It's very complicated. I know. Seems so, but it's a simple, trigger pull. End of a finger," I said. "Hey, I want to ask you guys something…"

"What?" Pumpkin Two said, "you wanna know how much

money you almost fucked us all out of, you prick bastard?"

The door busted open. It was Captain Richard Powell Dickerson. The two nervous high-heelers jittered behind him glaring in.

"Hey! HEY! Put that gun down, Rusty!" He leaped to my side, pointing a finger at me. "Put that down, you stupid fuck."

I straightened myself up and then, ever-so-slowly, laid the nine on the desk.

"You two nuts get the fuck out of here," Dickerson declared. "GO!"

"Yeah!' I echoed. "You two pumpkins get out of this patch!" I don't know what that meant. I just said it. Perhaps someday Val Kilmer will say it in a famous movie called Rusty Earp?

Powell backslapped me across my upper arm.

Cranston picked up his pistol.

"Light weight gun for a light weight player," I said.

"You shut up!" Powell yelled at little old me.

The Bobbsey Twins left, their fists, no doubt, painfully sore from me hitting them with my hard face so many times. Powell's eyes scoured the room and found a shelf still on the wall by a coffee machine and cleaning supplies. He tossed me a roll of paper towels. I caught it.

"Fix yourself up. We are gonna' get out of here, and we're walking down to my office," he told me. "Calmly, and without making a scene."

The paper blotted up my bloody snot. It felt like sandpaper on my cheeks.

"It's going to take a lot more than Mister Brawny to fix this face," I added.

The two ladies filed in, staring at me.

"Sorry ladies, but I had to file a citizen's complaint somewhere. They took me here," I said to them.

"Come on," Dickerson said.

In five minutes we were in Dickerson's plush office. He pointed to a chair in front of his desk, and I sat.

He stared at me.

"What?" I asked.

"What the hell have you been doing these last 9 years?"

"Drugs. Hookers on drugs."

"You look like it. You look like your father, for Christ's sake, Rusty. Right before he died at 70. I swear."

My...father? I hadn't thought about my father in years. Fourteen years. Like I never even had one.

"He's dead?"

"He died about 5 years ago."

"Oh."

"Don't you read the papers?"

"Not unless they start reporting the rise and falling price of street dope in the business section, that'll be a no."

"You seen your ex-wife?"

"No."

"You seen your kids? You know they're in college now?"

"No. I told you, Rich, I was busy doing drugs. If I go see Nance all she'll want is 14 years of child support. I can't do that."

"Linda still sees Nancy." Linda was Rich's wife. "Nancy is remarried now, Rusty. Your name does not come up. Trust me. And, she does not want or need child support from you."

"Oh, I trust ya."

"She gets your monthly disability check."

Disability check? Oh yeah. That.

"After you disappeared, a judge awarded it to her. I know that the money goes to send your daughters to college."

I nodded. I have a deep, dark secret about my wife, you know. One I cannot tell anyone. I certainly cannot tell Rich.

He would never believe me, and he would never believe another word I said to him. Then he wouldn't believe what I would tell him about Steverino. But, my wife is not my wife. I mean, my ex-wife is not my wife. I mean, my ex-wife is not my ex-wife. She is not the same woman. No, not in personality. Nope. The whole thing. Look, here's the deal. When I woke up from my coma? This dark-haired woman was sitting next to me. She started to cry when I woke up. She looked like an actress playing my wife in a movie. She looked a little like her, but she was absolutely not my wife.

She called out my name. "Rusty," she said. "Rusty," she screamed. My kids ran into the hospital room, and they hugged my arms. They were laughing, and they were happy. They were my kids. My real kids. But, she was not Nancy. She was a stranger. Why?

My real wife was waiting out in the hallway at the hospital. Oh yeah, I know this. When this actress left my room to tell people in the hall I was awake? Then I heard Nancy's voice in the hall telling them. THAT was my wife. That voice in the hall. She was excited and telling people I was awake. THAT was her. Then, then in one minute this same actress walked back into the room again and hugged me, pretending to be Nancy. Why was Nancy sending an actress into my room to pretend to be her? Why would she hide in the hall? Why would she do that to me? I was shot! I wanted to see her. Find out what happened to me, but she wouldn't come into the room? She must have hired an actress to play her? Why would she do this? And my kids were in on this, too! They played like they loved this stranger like their real mother. How could they do this? But I could never tell Rich this because I cannot explain this. No one can. Why do this to me? I have talked to my real wife on the phone a few times. This is her voice. I have begged her to stop these actions to me. She just cried and called me crazy. She just never wanted to see me again. I don't like her, and I don't like this actress, and I don't like my kids who pretended this woman was their mother. My kids were in on this! Something is not right about this. A conspiracy to drive me away and drive me crazy. I can't explain it.

And Rich would think I am crazy, too, and he would not believe anything else I told him. But, I have a secret about my wife no one believes and no one understands. I haven't thought about this in years because I was too busy. My secret.

And I have never told anyone this either, but that is the first time I saw General Grant. He was sitting in the corner of my room, in his army uniform, legs crossed, watching me. Grant's picture was the last thing the old Rusty here saw before the old Rusty died on the steps of Grant's tomb, and about the first thing I saw when I woke up from my coma.

My eyes fell on Rich and Linda's picture on the wall. Their kids. Toothy smiles from expensive, up-town orthodontists. It was an admin office wall for sure. Working street cops and working detectives can't afford to have pretty pictures of their wife and kids on their desks and on their walls where street scumbags can see them, can slobber all over them and comment on them. Can make plans on them and threaten them and even kill them. The working-class cop and the case agent dick hides his family. The admin displays them as if they managed a tire store.

"You've done well for yourself, El Capitan," I said.

"Why are you here?" He cut to the chase.

"Long story. You got any whiskey in here?"

Rich sighed, went to a cabinet and pulled out a bottle of Jack Daniels and two coffee cups. He handed me one and splashed two fingers worth of Jack in the mug. He did the same for himself. I looked at my cup. It had a cartoon drawing on it of a homicide detective pulling his hair out, seated at his desk. The line under him read, "Homicide. Our day begins when your day ends."

"You STILL have this homicide cup?" I asked.

"Yeah," he half-smiled and sat. An occasional cup o' Jack was not a new ritual for Rich and me in those thrilling days of yesteryear.

I took two of the Lipshitz pain pills from my pocket, tossed them in my sore, busted-up mouth and sipped the Jack. It leeched into the open wounds in my mouth and stung like Drano. Ever get beaten so bad that the inside of your mouth is cut up?

"Why do these guys around here hate you so much? Why do they want to beat you and talk about killing you on sight?" he asked me.

The pain pills, or the whiskey, seemed to kick in? Something kicked in. My dad kicked in? Like a ghost or something. I leaned forward and looked my old friend dead in the eyes and a voice came from my mouth that was also like an old friend to me, a voice I hadn't heard from me in a long time. And, it sounded just a bit like my dear ol' dad's, come to think of it.

"Rich, ever hear of the Five Apes?" I asked him.

"Five…. Apes? A little. Something."

I stared at his face. His eyes. He hadn't. I continued. "In the 1990s, there was a caper to smuggle heroin in from China. The heroin, and then later cocaine, came in ships, inside cat food bags. The dope bags came in the middle of boatloads of shipments of normal cat food. The dope bags were specially marked…"

"Cat food? Just a few years ago…"

"I know. I know. Cats were just dying from Chinese-made, cat food. The governments said it was from dirty Chinese factories and the wrong ingredients. Cats eat rats and that doesn't kill them, right? Come on. Cover-up bullshit. Mistakes were made in China, and some product got mixed up with the regular cat food machines. Some of the cutting materials got mixed in, too. The results - dead American cats. Over-dosed cats. You can kill our kids, but you can't kill our cats!" I smiled. I'll bet it was a crazy smile because Powell just looked at me funny.

I took another sip and it hit like lava. I continued.

"Me, Agent David Williams and Agent Anthony Longoria of the DEA fell into this operation. The original snitch on this was my guy. A Chinese-American guy. A low-level guy we caught in a jam slugging his daughter around, and he turned for me in this deal. He translated a lot of the day-to-day for the smugglers and the dock workers running those cat food bags."

"And you didn't tell me this?"

"No. No, I did not tell you. First off, buddy, this is after we worked together, years after, and I was in Organized Crime. You know, you were just another guy on the homicide squad back then. I was in O.C. That 'need to know' thing? And, well, because the operation was inside the police department." I thumped his desk. "Cops were in on the take up and down the chain of command. Shit, Rich, some nights, narcotics and organized crime cops helped unload the cat food bags from ships. I was under strict orders from the Chief's Office, the CIA…"

"The CIA?"

"The CIA and the DEA told me not to breathe a word of it to anyone. They told me it was too big to handle just here in New York. They told me that they would work all this out with Interpol, track the heroin and coke to its source in mainland China, and all I would have to do was turn over my informant to them. They told me to just sit back and read Time Magazine and, in about one year, I'd read all about the big international drug busts and all the dirty cops caught in the ring. I did just that."

"No big busts."

"No big busts. But that traffic ceased for a while, anyway. Now it all comes in somehow and somewhere else. Dog food, maybe. North Carolina? But, I do know this. In one year's time, Agent Anthony Longoria was dead, shot in his car on a stakeout. And David Williams of state narcotics, stabbed in the throat while fishing in the Finger Lakes."

"Yeah," Rich remembered.

"My Chinese snitch was dead, too. Tossed off a high rise in Queens. And six months after all that, I got shot in the stomach."

"But the Mob shot you? Al was a mobster."

"The Mob shot me, but people in this building…1PP… the police paid them," I said.

Rich stared at me like I was crazy again. I know crazy, and this was not crazy.

"And Cranston and Macelroy?" Rich asked.

"In on it. I know most every one of them. Or, I use to know everyone."

"Who the fuck are these people?"

"The Five Apes, Rich. Ever hear the story of the Five Apes?" I asked again.

"No, I told you. What the fuck do five fucking apes have to do with anything?"

"It's a nickname. A funny nickname to them. A true experiment. You start with five apes in a cage. In the cage, you hang a banana on a string and put stairs under it. Before long an ape will climb up to get the banana. As soon as the ape touches the banana, the keepers spray all the apes with freezing, cold water. All of them. After a while, another ape makes a try for the banana. All the apes are sprayed with freezing water. Now, if another ape tries to climb the stairs for the banana, all the other apes in the cage stop it. Then these scientists see it and they quit spraying the water. Even though no water sprays the apes, they still beat the ape that reaches for the banana."

I sipped the whiskey. Rich was engrossed. Confused, but engrossed.

"You getting this picture? Take out an ape, put in a new ape. Monkey tries for the banana, and the other four apes kick his ass. After replacing the fourth and fifth of the original apes there weren't any of the original apes who were ever sprayed with ice water. But, no ape ever again approaches the banana anymore. Do? And you get a beating. Why? Because that's the way it's always been around here…in the cage."

"What the fuck?"

"Hey, I got beat today, huh? These cops? They nick-named themselves 'The Five Apes?' Like a club. A secret club. One night on surveillance, we taped some of them telling stories on the docks. One of them told the story of the Five Apes. Their origin, to some new guys. We'd even seen some of them wearing t-shirts and even rings with five apes on them. Like it's a joke."

"Their point?"

"Oh, I get their point, their joke. After a while? Who knows the rules in the cage? Who knows why the rules were ever even made? What rules count or don't count? Cop rules. Crook rules. The law. Life is either an ass-whop-ping by the biggest, hairy fists, or not. Life in the cage."

"The cage."

"Life in the cage."

"How many of them? These five apes?"

"Fifty of them. A hundred. Who knows now? Who are the originals? Do you really want to know?" I stood up suddenly. Stressed out. I walked around the office. "You think I will tell you? Telling on them is killing you, my friend." I waved him off and crashed back in the chair, rubbing my hands together. My hands suddenly felt like they had a ton of callous on them.

"It is best you never know who they are," I told him. I inspected my hands thoroughly.

"How high up?"

"Street cops. Dicks. Admin. Some politicians. Some Mafia. Players with no hearts. Life-takers." I pointed to the photo of Rich and Linda with my finger. "You don't wanna know." I started picking on the biggest callous. If I could get the first chunk off. Just a small chuck? Maybe I could start peeling it all off in strips. You know, like jerky? Like beef jerky.

"These Five Apes guys? That why you are here?" Rich asked.

"Nah," I worked my tender tongue around my sore mouth. I wasn't too sure why I was there, really. Come to think of it. Maybe I should get back to Jersey and get bombed? A wave of nervousness washed over me. Actually it was cold fright. Ice cold. Like I was the one suddenly reaching for that banana.

I leaned forward again. "Listen, Rich, you remember the China Doll case? The United Nations, Chinese Embassy, the Chinese diplomat's wife raped and killed? Upper East Side?"

"Yeah…I do."

"We arrested Steverino Downing for that."

"Yeah,"

"From Harlem."

"Yeah!" Rich's head bobbed up and down.

"Yeah. Yeah. Why'd he do that?"

"Why? Well…sex, I guess."

"Why did…" and I coughed, suddenly, but it gushed out into a damn crying fit. A fit! I don't know why the fuck I started to cry. I just did. Rich looked at me stunned. I still had some Mr. Brawny paper towels in my coat pocket and pulled them out. I blew my nose. I sniveled and squirmed like a silly fool in the electric chair for a few seconds. Breathe. Breathe deep.

"I...got word, that...that the guy? Steverino... didn't do this," I said. I could hardly speak.

"You got word."

"I got word."

"That's like, like over...what...12 years ago, 14? Who the fuck cares, Rusty?"

I was like...now vomiting tears at this point. Must have been loud. Someone knocked on the door and opened it without permission. Was I that loud? Rich told the person at the door that everything was okay and to leave.

"You need drug rehab," he said.

"Drug rehab ain't gonna cut it. I need the Spanish Inquisition," I said.

"When was the last time you took a hit of something?" he asked.

"I don't know. Maybe two weeks ago."

"Two weeks! Rusty you can't be a drug addict," Rich said.

Two weeks? Two weeks since Al called me from Upstate to meet me.

"Two weeks," I said. "I have to be in some kind of withdrawal. I mean, I have been seeing shit. Ghosts and shit. I feel like hell. My guts are inside out. Can't think straight." I took a nibble on the callous that was on the back of my thumb. Maybe I could get a chunk started that way?

"You've been like that since the coma."

"Coma?" I whispered. I blew my nose, which started bleeding again, damnit.

"You were in a coma for four months at Bellevue, Rusty. After the shooting! That one bullet went through your guts and the other into your head."

"My head?" I mumbled. Oh, yeah. My head shot. I…the other round…sometimes I forget about my head shot. I can't seem to remember that about my head shot, just my stomach shot. A coma? That what I was in when I woke up and my wife's actress was next to me. Oh yeah. I was in a coma.

"Rusty, one of the bullets hit the top of your head," Rich explained. "It traveled around your brain. The doctors said…the doctors said you have some impact damage. Some…brain damage, Rusty."

"Brain damage," I repeated slowly with a hollow voice, staring at the floor. Nice carpet down there. Berber was it? Nice. I saw my gray face in Damon's big, shiny black shoes on my feet, all distorted like a fun house mirror. I felt like that. If I think about those bullets? It's hard. I think I can think about them, you know? Like I can really grasp the bullets that hit me. It was like a ball peen hammer hit my skull. Ever feel something like a hammer clocking you on the head? When I do think about it, my mind kind of fogs out. It must feel like going - I don't know – the beginning of going catatonic or something. My mind kind of collapses onto itself. Folds onto itself. I have trouble breathing.

"Rusty!"

See, it was happening again. I was folding in. I looked up at Rich. He was half-seated on the desk next to me. How'd he get there so fast?

"They are gonna' execute him next month," I said. Babbled, actually.

"Who…who in the fuck cares about Steverino? You know what Rusty? Maybe you are not a drug addict. Maybe you are a mental case first and take drugs second?"

"Ahhh, the Gold, the Silver or the Bronze? I always thought it was all a race to the finish. Ever wonder, ever think about why the China Doll was buried in Connecticut, Rich? The only death penalty state around here?" I asked.

"WHO cares?"

"Think about that crime, Rich, come on!" I said in exasperation. "Think about it. The woman was killed in her house. A handy neighbor identifies Steverino Downing as carrying a body-sized, rolled up carpet out of the house. To Connecticut he goes? Not the Hudson River? The Jersey swamps? A million places closer. Homeboy goes to…Connecticut?"

"So?"

"So, it stinks."

"You came over the river, over here, walked in here, after eight years, where dozens of cops want to beat you and maybe kill you, over Steverino Downing's pending execution?"

"No. Yes. I don't know. Look. What I wanna know..." The tears dried up like a vacuum, and my throat opened up. That ol' voice came back. "I wanna know who that neighbor was? Where is he now? I wanna know who tipped off the locals in Bridgeport about the body site. Is there any evidence left on the case for a DNA comparison? I want to know the name of Steverino's attorney. I wanna know who the prosecutor was."

Rich stared at me. "You're serious?"

"I will come back tomorrow at…"

"Noooo. NO! You will not come back here," he ordered. "Oh no. I swear, if I didn't see Mac and Cranston working you over, I wouldn't believe a word you said, you sick fuck… Five Apes!" He pulled a business card from his desk and wrote a number on the back. "Here, call my cell number…"

"Write that on a piece of paper, will ya'? I can't be caught with a cop's business card in my pocket. Ever! You kidding me?"

He did. I took it and shoved it in my coat pocket. I wrote my Wal-Mart phone number on another piece of paper I found on his desk.

I looked into his eyes. They were Rich's eyes, and they never changed. I smiled.

"I never should of come here," I said. "You are in enough trouble just entertaining me here in your office with your...your whiskey and Brawny paper towels."

I pushed the coffee cup of booze on the desk away from me. "I never should have done this to you. I didn't know jerk-offs like Mac and Cranston would be around so close, to make me so fast."

"You need to see a doctor," Rich said.

"I'll be fine," I said as I rolled up a small section of paper towel and shoved it on the outside of my lower left gum. "It'll stop bleeding. All I got is rust in my bloodstream."

"No, I mean a head doctor, a shrink."

"What? The department shrink? I've got rust on my brains, too. A shrink can't fix what's already shrunk. I will call you in three hours? Or you call me. Get me started with Steverino's lawyer first. Do not walk me out of here. You can't be seen with me again."

I left the office. I could only imagine how Rich felt. He had to think I was insane. Brain damage he said. A bear. A bear rants. Aberrant behavior is what the stone docs at Easter Island said about me. And what about these calluses growing like mushrooms on my hands. I needed a knife to hack them off!

Rich's secretary stared at me. She must have heard me crying like a baboon and looked into the office. I stopped and looked back at her. My swollen face and the towel rolled inside my mouth made me feel like Brando in "The Godfather."

"Tattaglia? Tattaglia's a pimp." I growled at her. "It was Barzeni."

She just stared at me. She seemed frightened. Wha? What? She never saw that movie?

Now. What did I say I was going to do next?

CHAPTER 6
LAYERING

Flushing Queens Express. I took a dark subway ride with flashing passes of above ground daylight visible through shafts and grated metal plates. Lights like this can bother me. Make me dizzy. I slumped over and stared at the soiled floor of the subway. Stain upon stain. Like blood spatter evidence. Splash upon splash. Tricky evidence. Blood dropped one way atop blood dropped another way. Which way does the evidence go? It's a layer on layer investigation.

Sticky. How many feet touched this very floor? Millions and millions of stinking feet, I'll bet. Soiled soles. Gum. Trash. You name it. Picked up, pee-stained drops on the floor under urinals of filthy subway station bathrooms. Picked up and carried off everywhere on shoes. Carried here at my feet.

I fought two skels on a subway floor like this many years ago, on a robbery stakeout. Wrestled around with them on these floors. My face touched these floors. Rolled all over them. I shot one in the leg, and the back-up team grabbed the other. A skel is just an old NYPD nickname for skeleton or a drug addict. Was I a skel now, too? Rich said I was not a drug addict crazy from drugs. He said I was a crazy man who happened to use drugs. Now that's some layering.

General Grant was ten rows down watching me. He was President once too, you know, but today he was dressed like a general. He always visits me dressed like a general with layered clothing. Winter jacket. Uniform underneath. He carried a cane today, too. Grant never says anything to me when I see him. He just stares at me. I don't mind him. When you die? What set of clothes do you wear? Who gets to pick? What do you wear in Heaven? Your favorite duds? Is it your coffin clothes? Your death clothes?

I've seen my blood in pictures. It tells how I fell at Grant's Tomb. My body was gone. "Removed" from the site, as they say. But the blood spatter remained. It shows how I fell. How I squirmed. Where the EMT's sat and kneeled around me.

I shut my eyes and went down deep. Right away, I saw Alphonso the Crepe Hanger. I saw Louis Geampo-lova shoot me again. I went that deep, that fast. I was on the steps of Grant's Tomb near Riverside. I was meeting someone. Who? Can't remember but it was a phony, set-up anyway. Because Al set it up, and Al showed up. Al and Louie. It wasn't too late that night. Maybe 8-ish. I knew Al and Louie right away when I saw them. They started up the steps and the jerkoffs never stopped glaring at me. They were walking tip-offs to trouble.

I felt my mouth wince in pain, and it woke me up. Grant was still there staring at me. I was bearing down on my teeth. Grinding them. My eyelids felt heavy again. My head slumped over. Out. And then the steps. This part on the Tomb steps was the really bad part, the bad moment; and I hated it, because I knew I could have done something right then and there on the Tomb steps to change all this. If I had just moved my friggin' snail body to the left a few inches! If I had just dropped back and pulled my gun. If... anything! One step, and my whole life would have been different. A few inches.

The train rocked me back into its rhythm. I wonder how many people had cried in this subway? How many tears hit that soiled floor and mixed with the urine and the grease and the grit? And every single day, people just walk all over it. And the rubber dries it out. Crushes it out to a squeak.

Louie opened his jacket, and it just wasn't natural. I just knew he was pulling a gun. I pulled mine. He hadn't spent a thousand hours at the range drawing and shooting, but I had. His tan jacket became a blur as I focused in on the front sights of my gun. That was a 20 plus yard shot. But ol' Louie was drawing too and hit me. He hit me in my stomach first. Low. And ...and I bent over. I bent over, or so they told me. My head was low. He hit me in my head. Square in the top of my head. You can't dodge such a thing. Such a very fast thing. A bullet. It hit me like a good swing of a hammer. And Rusty died there, but the meat puppet moves on.

When I was shot, I thought I heard a horn honk, and it felt like someone clapped glass ashtrays on my ears. Someone told me later it was pressure in and all around my head. The shock. The ball-peen hammer strike to my head. The world went all sideways, like you see from a dropped movie camera. I laid on my back. They say I shot my gun until it ran empty. Maybe that saved my sorry life? I didn't watch. Couldn't. I was disconnected. My arms and legs wrangled all around. I lost them. They weren't mine anymore. My head twisted up to the Grant Museum. Then, I saw Mr. Ulysses S. Grant sitting on the steps just above me. He had a stogie in his hand, and he was dressed like a Civil War general in the winter. He looked at me, shaking his head. He looked at me. "These bad boys wear blue," he said.

I wanted to tell him it was the Mob, not NYPD that shot me. But in the end, Grant was right. How did he know so soon?

My brain now works in splashing layers, too, like crust on this subway. Splash this way. Splash that way. I have several things going on at once. Like old voices. New voices. Like that. My brain likes to forget about the bullet to the head I took; but I can remember it sometimes. It's always raining in my head...

My phone rang, and I yanked it from my coat pocket.

"Rusty?"

"Yeah."

"It's Rich. Steverino's lawyer has been dead for seven years. Nothing suspicious. He was real old. Like 80 or something."

"Thanks, Rich. Find out the rest for me."

I put the phone away. No lawyer. Dead. No one pushing appeals. No one speaking out. No advocate. But, I knew just what to do as the subway pulled into the Port Authority Terminal. Get off! I'd been riding it back and forth for hours. One end of the line and back again. I wanted to drive Cranston and Macelroy crazy. The sons of bitch pumpkin heads had followed me since I left One Police Plaza.

The train stopped. Doors opened.

I waited.

I waited.

I waited. The sound of the doors about to close...

I suddenly leaped from the train just before the doors shushed close. It clipped the heel of my shoe, well...Damon's shoe. I would guess the dynamic duo were a few cars down and stepped off the train and watched everyone leave, didn't see me leave, and waited until the last second to jump back in, the doors clipping their heels too, but the wrong way. Wrong-way, peach-fuzz! Ha! I even tricked the General because he stayed on the train. Hard to trick the supernatural! He sat there calmly in his seat, smoking his cigar.

I rode the escalators up to the lobby and stepped off to the right, turned and barely peeked around the wall. No Cran-ston. No Macelroy. HA! I hoped they enjoyed the express run. I made for the bank of public computer terminals in the lobby. One on a back row. I used some of the dear Missus Lillian Lipshitz's money to turn on the internet.

"Freedom Science Foundation," I typed. The webpage popped up. There it was. Downtown Manhattan, the largest public-funded group of specialized lawyers in the country using DNA and any other means, to solve old cases and to free innocent, incarcerated people. A newspaper report said.

All lead by a South African fireball of a woman named Sadame Prevell. A lawyer during the days of apartheid.

She was famous, in this business anyway. I could ac-tually just walk to the foundation from there. Steverino needed a new lawyer.

I strutted across the terminal toward a wall of restau-rants and into a Chili's. Ordered a steak, fries and a coke. Hmmmm, it was good and settled my stomach, even though I ate quickly. I felt normal sitting there. Whatever that means. Good food! Fast! I stuck the steak knife in my coat pocket, paid and left the terminal.

But, I had one more stop before the Freedom Science Foundation. Two blocks downtown is where Cranston and Macelroy parked their unmarked, detective car to follow me into the station. I may have been reborn a few years ago? But I wasn't born yesterday. And I was once a member of the most elite squad of one of the largest agencies in the world. Did I tell you that? I know how the bad boys in blue think, operate, plan and fuck up. I walked up to their car.

Poof. Poof. Poof. Poof. Four NYPD, CID car tires nice and flat, courtesy of a Chili's steak knife. I figured I'd keep the knife in case I got the lucky chance to poof a few things more later on tonight. The day was still young.

Off, to the Science…the Science…ahhh, where was I going again?

CHAPTER 7
FREEDOM'S JUST ANOTHER
WORD FOR LOBOTOMY

I pushed opened the glass double doors of the Freedom Science Foundation and took a seat in the lobby to get my bearings. I needed to make a plan because it was crazy crowded in there. I had the feeling I was now inside a rectory or a holy place. The smell of the place, don't get me wrong it didn't stink, but it smelled of new paint, furniture, cologne, clothes from dry cleaners. A power smell. It hit my busted, swollen nose like an insect fog. The lobby was packed with busy men and women in lawyer clothes, and I was dizzy from it. There were chairs off to the side, and I had to sit down, hypnotized by all the weaving motion of clean, smart people.

Within all this motion I saw just one face. One. It was like a statue. Still. Perfectly still. A black, tall woman with blackish-gray colored skin and a large gray afro. Circa like the 1960s. And she was in her late 50s, Early 60s. She was slim, she was fit. It was like someone jammed an immoveable black and white statue down into a tidal wave. It didn't budge. And to further freak me out? She was staring right back at me. It was the Sadame Prevell. We just looked at each across this marble lobby.

Then she walked through it all, at a different pace slower than everyone else and right up to me.

"How are you today, sir?" she asked me. She had that odd British mix accent of an Afrikaner. British? African? Wha?

"Detached."

"Detached?" she repeated. She seemed surprised at that answer. Why not? It surprised me, but I was being perfectly honest with her.

I nodded.

"You are Rusty…Rusty? Rusty the police investigator that…"

"Was shot in the head." I finished her sentence for her.

"Yes. The detective that was shot in the head at Grant's Tomb years ago. It's no wonder you feel detached, detective," she said.

"I am not a detective anymore."

"What are you then?" She eyed me up and down as I stood there in Damon's suit.

"I am in an investigation. Not the investigator. Not… detecting."

"Hmm, I see. And can we…help you with something?"

"Yes, with an innocent man that is about to be killed."

She just stared at me. No expression. Like a beautiful, marble statue stuck fast in time. We are all moving. Not her.

"I am not a detective anymore. I am detached from that."

"Okay, but you were once a very good detective. I read all about you. And I trust that is why you are here today, because you are still attached to the good part of all that." She raised an eyebrow and looked me over.

She was a beautiful work of art, and I just looked at it. I mean it.

"My name's is Sadame Prevell. Everyone calls me Sad."

"I understand." I thought it sad that they call her Sad. Is that like a karmic joke or something?

"Come on back to my office with me. Come on."

I followed her across the lobby, down a hall and into an office. Inside, the room was decorated in African art like in a '60s blaxploitation movie. But I already knew Sad was from South African. You see I read about her, too. She was once a medical doctor and now a lawyer. A radical liberator. A voice. An aide for Nelson Mandela in the South African government. And then she moved to New York City in the late 1990s. In 2005 she was hired to run this freedom law firm that does one service. In a nutshell? It frees innocent people from their nutshells. It was financed by the upper crusty rich, the kind of crust people like me or Steverino don't have.

"Have Peter come in," she said into an intercom on her desk. She sat. I sat. She stared.

"You are into DNA. That's what you do?" I asked, kind of nervously.

"That is a lot of what we do. I do."

"There is a man in Connecticut on death row, who has been convicted of killing the China Doll. He is innocent," I told her.

"How exactly do you know he is innocent?"

"I don't know how I know," I answered.

"Well, I remember the China Doll case." Her eyes scanned me up and down. "I remember the China Doll murder, yes, and I ..ahhh, Mister Rusty, the pinky on your right hand."

"Yeah?"

"It is twitching. Does that always happen?"

"I don't know." I shrugged. I looked at my pinky. Damn thing was moving like mad, like it was detached from my brain and was trying to escape. Wild. My little wayward finger was bending in positions it shouldn't. Like a cramp, ass backward.

This guy Peter came in. A long-nosed hulk with greased black hair. Turtleneck under a sport coat. He was packing under that. Shoulder holster. He stood off to the side of Sad's desk, looking at me. He was like...Dutch African... British. How do I know? I just knew. He was a white guy, by the way, this hulk guy.

"Hmmm. The left side of your face doesn't seem to have any muscle movement. When you blink? Your eyelids are not synchronized. Do you have a doctor? A neurologist?"

"No."

"Are you on any medication, Rusty?"

"Just medications of mass destruction."

Sad turned sideways to the large computer screen on her desk that I could see. She typed on a keypad. Up on the screen popped a picture of me back when I was a cool breeze. NYPD days. I remember the photo. It was taken at a crime scene and was used by the local papers as a standard stock photo when they needed one of me. Hey, I was looking good. Suit and tie. Coiffed. I even looked a little bit like Russell Crowe way back when. Now I look like Mickey Rooney after a car wreck. Sad read the pages. She clicked and read and clicked and read. I saw pictures of me. Narcotics unit. Homicide. Organized crime. News and news. A picture of me and my wife, the papers used after I was shot in the cranium. Then I saw pictures of me after the shooting flash on the screen. A hospital shot. Me with my head bandaged in court. The medal picture – yeah – the PD even gave me a medal for being shot. I was totally spaced out then at the ceremony. I wonder where that medal is? I probably ate it on a ham and cheese sandwich.

Then she turned, looked at me and stared.

"If you are wondering," I said, "none of the guys in those pictures are me anymore."

She pursed her lips, squinted and turned back to the screen.

"It says here that you were something of a rising rock star in the police department."

"I arose. I was shot. I arose to be shot. The rock…and then the rock fell on me."

The China Doll popped up on the screen. Pictures of her. News stories. The case. The cracking of the case. The trial of the case. The conviction of the case. Sad pointed and clicked through it all. She blew up a newspaper picture of Steverino.

"Yeah, yeah, that's the guy. That's Steverino Downing. He's the guy who is innocent."

"Why is he innocent?"

"A guy told me. One of the two guys that shot me. He was in jail upstate with Steverino's son. The son said his dad was innocent."

"Okay," she said in a condescending tone. "Might there be any evidence that he is innocent?"

"Not yet."

"Not yet?"

"Not…yet. That's why I am here. The Chinese Doll was married to a Chinese diplomat named Bo Zoup, right? It seemed to us, back then, it was like a simple sex crime and murder. With a few very fast and lucky breaks. Way too fast and way too lucky. Steverino was arrested. Tucked away. We moved on. Then I got promoted to the Organized Crime Unit. I was working on a big-league heroin import case. Heroin from China. I found out this Bo Zoup was involved in this somehow. Some way. Shipping. Tariffs. Trade imbalance. When I learned this, it was still just a big drug case. The Feds took the whole investigation over. I was out of it. Our unit was out. They had big plans with this case. Big promises to me. But I realized…"

Dammit, I started to choke up again. I leaned forward in the chair and squeezed my fist to control my eyes.

"...I thought years later that the old China Doll case was funky. You know? How could it all be so simple? A guy in the neighborhood kills her in her home? Something wasn't right. And then...and then, the big Federal import case disappeared. Agents involved stared dying. And I was shot down, too. Only I didn't die all the way. They killed my brain, but I am still walking around."

She stared at me.

"I am the last one. The only one."

She nodded.

"You ever hear of the Five Apes?" I asked.

Sad looked at Peter the Hulk. It was like a firecracker went off in her eyeballs.

"Call Dr. Suliman. Tell him I have an emergency patient...."

"Hey!" I cried out. "I am not here for me. We have an emergency all right, but it's a death sentence on an innocent man. I don't need a doctor. I need an appeals lawyer who will kick ass."

"Mister Rusty," Sad said. "Your brains are spinning like a broken slot machine. Until I can get your head straight, I can't pull the handle and come up a winner."

She looked back up at Peter, "Call Suliman and get us in for this evening, if he can, please? Then get my driver and the car around back as soon as possible."

"Right away," Peter said. I caught the accent. I TOLD you he was South African! He walked across the room to another desk, sat and started using the phone.

"You're coming with us, too, Peter. No ice hockey for you tonight. Sorry."

"The clinic is in upstate New York," she turned to me and said.

I stood up to get out of there right then. No way I am....

"Sit down, Rusty."

I sat back down. Queen's orders. My damn pinky banging away on my thigh like a '60s rock band drummer overdosing.

"An MRI?" She said. "An exam. Some medication. You know, just some of the things you do after one's been shot in the head. Your nose is very bruised and swollen."

"Thanks for noticing. Yeah, two of NYPD's finest beat the snot out of me this morning. Some old friends saying hello."

"Why did they do that?"

"They can't have me around. They can't have me waking up. That's why I'm in here with you. It's all about why I am here. If they see me walking and talking and hanging around? I become a new version of an old problem."

"Well, Peter here? He is a former South African Commando and police detective. He was also a bodyguard for Nelson Mandela. Peter will help protect you from these officers."

I just looked at his face. Expressionless, as he hung up the phone.

"What caliber you got there?" I looked at his covered armpit.

"Forty-Five."

"What size knife do you have in your pocket?" he asked me.

"Chili's steak." I realized that my jacket, damn, I mean Damon's jacket side was lying over the chair arm and well, the shape of my knife was evident.

"Good eyes, hulk-man."

"I'd like to see it closer," he said. He talked funny, emphasizing his "Ts" and "Ds."

I took the knife out, and he cautiously took it. He walked away with it. I was cool with that. Anyway, I could kill a man with an eyelash, so I am never really weapon-less.

Sad watched the little transaction with her big brown eyes.

"Peter will protect you. You won't need a knife," she said.

Right. She said there were some things to do when one is shot in the head? That "one" being - yours truly.

Was I shot in the head? Or the belly? Yeah, yeah, head, too. I grabbed my radical pinky and my ring finger and squeezed them tight with my right hand. My little piggy just wouldn't stop trying to squirm off to market. It felt like a muscle-bound worm having a seizure. Hang on! Don't escape.

"Can I have some of that scotch tape?" I pointed to it on her desk.

She pushed it over to me. I took off some long pieces and taped the two fingers together.

"Oh and yes, Rusty, I have heard of the Five Apes," she said.

Okay…she did. Okay…now…are we going somewhere?

CHAPTER 8
SHOCKING TREATMENTS

A long black limo pulled up in the back. The long black lady named Sad got in the back-left side, and Peter the Hulk and I got into the right side. Peter sat facing us in the back. That kind of limo. The driver was a very dark-skinned black man. I can't remember if I was ever inside a limo in my life. This life or last. We pulled out into Manhattan traffic.

Sad talked on her cell phone. Peter opened a New York Times newspaper. The sports page.

"Peter, you play Rugby?"

"Yes, I did."

"You knew Nelson Mandela?"

"Yes, I did."

"You like him?"

"Yes, I did." He smiled like he knew he said the same 'I did' answer three times. "He did a lot to change my country. It was needed. It was welcome."

I really like the way this guy said his Ts and Ds. Like he was gulping or something.

"Rusty, did you know that I was a medical doctor in South Africa?" Sad interrupted us.

"Yeah. Doctor and lawyer." She could have been a model, too.

"I went to medical school in London. I am also a doctor now here in New York State. Much of my work was on the human brain."

"Okay."

"I have been on the phone with Dr. Suliman. He was a doctor with me in South Africa. He is a groundbreaking specialist in the treatment of human brain injuries. He's made many advances."

Advances. Toward her or toward needed medical discoveries? She smiled slightly when she talked to me. What a…what a perky, saucy smile, curled off to the side of her face. She was selling me something. And I was buying.

"We are going to give you some important medication right away. Are you allergic to any drugs?"

"I've never met a drug I didn't like."

"Good. Rusty, we are going to administer some treatment to you tonight. Have you heard of shock treatments?"

"Shock treatments," I repeated, shocked a little. She was selling me shock treatments. All with that little saucy smile?

"Electro convulsive therapy. ETC. Yes. There are many new advances in shock therapy. Dr. Suliman is a leading neurologist in this field. We are headed there, and we are going to give you some tonight."

"Drugs and electricity. In that order."

"In that order. Rusty will you roll your sleeve up?" She reached into a black leather bag on the floor beside her.

I did. I took Damon's jacket off and rolled up Damon's shirt sleeve. I took off Damon's belt and wrapped it around Da – I mean my bicep. Gave it a yank. This surprised Sad and Peter. She had a needle prepped and just looked at me.

I stuck the end of the belt in my mouth, pulled it hard and mumbled, "Gimme. Gimme."

Her eyes widened and she handed me the spike. I gave it a little push to clear any bubbles and hit a big forearm vein. I undid my rig and handed her the needle back.

"You've done this before?"

"A time or thousand," I nodded my head.

She capped and wrapped the needle in some cloth like a good little doctor.

"Destroy that," I warned about the needle. "WHOA!" I uttered. "I feel it. I feel that shit." It rippled right over my scalp like stampeding cats.

MY phone rang. I scrambled for Damon's jacket and got the phone.

"Yeah?"

"Rusty? Rich. The neighbor that testified that he saw Steverino carry something body sized out of the house. Delafasio. He testified that it was a rolled-up rug. Remember? The rug was buried with the body."

"Yeah! Delafasio!"

"He still lives in the same house."

"Give me everything on him. DOB. Everything."

"You got a pen?"

"Don't need a pen. Go with it."

Sad rummaged through her purse to get a pen and paper. She handed it to me as I repeated all the info Rich told me out loud. I waved her off.

"Okay. Okay. Anything on the Connecticut witness?"

"Confidential. It was a Crime Stoppers tip. Don't know about the tipster."

"Okay. Okay. Yeah. Crime Stoppers. Caller was paid $1,000 in a secret transaction. Get a rundown on the evidence left on the case. We need any DNA we can possibly get. Rich, we probably need to see all the evidence anyway."

"You'll need a court order."

"No problem. Get it ready. A lawyer will be forthcoming. Find the Mister China Doll!"

"Bo Zoup? Where are you now?"

"You don't want to know. On the move." I hit the goodbye button. Thinking about all this.

You need to write that down?" Sad asked.

"No, Sad," I said calmly. Too calmly. Too collectively. Maybe it was that needle of juice. I found that old voice in me again. "Since I was shot in the head. I have some kind of photographic memory. If I see or hear something. I can remember it if I want to."

"Oh."

"I see dead people," I added.

"You see…"

"Not a lot of dead people. Not like the kid in the Bruce Willis movie." My voice was sad talking to Sad. "Just one. Sitting right next to you, Peter. Right there?" I pointed. "Is General Ulysses S. Grant."

"From Grant's Tomb?" Sad said.

"From Grant's Tomb. What good is a tomb if you don't stay in it?" I asked Grant. He didn't answer. "He is just one of my lousy curses. You don't want to know the others. What I've done. But listen, we need everything we can dig up on Delafasio. Every little thing."

"We'll never know who the Crime Stoppers witness was," Sad said.

"Ohhh, we'll see what I see. Do the people in South Africa play rough? Do they play the law rough like rugby, Peter?"

"They can."

"You seen rough?"

"Yeah."

"You play rough? Play rough cop in South Africa?"

"Yeah."

"How bout you Sad lady. You play rough?"

"Rusty, I helped South Africa climb out of Apartheid. I freed hundreds of innocent people in prison from murder and torture any way I could. Justice knows no one country, or even one set of laws. The local law is one tool to get justice. I play rough for justice."

"I like you more and more, Sad lady." That shot of whatever it was set my mind back a few levels into the basement, and this basement was a crash pad. "Wheeeww. I'm feeling that medicine down deep." I sat back in the limo seat.

"Playing rough for justice," I repeated in a sigh.

"Rusty where do you live?"

"On the lone prairie…" I felt a song coming on.

"Oh bury me not on the lone prairie. Where the grapes of wrath won't throw their pits on me."

"You actually have a pretty, good voice, Rusty," Sad said.

Peter the Hulk was grinning. I did sing great actually and put my all into every lyric when I did sing. I am not shy at all about my singing. I finished the whole cowboy song with my special phrasing.

"I don't live…anywhere. On the streets," I said. "I have had some houses and apartments I've stayed at. But you might say that I am homeless."

"Okay. Well, you will be staying in a very nice hotel for a bit. Until we can unwrap what is going on."

"We need every scrap of information on Delafasio we can get. You never know what we might find. He is a paid-off liar in the first degree. We only have so much time left. Can you…can you make some high-powered, rough calls for justice?"

"Yes," Sad said.

I yawned and sank deeper in the seat. Grant was gone now when I looked for him. Gone in just a flash. Maybe evaporated back into his tomb? You know how these ghosts travel. Here a minute. Gone the next. I rested my head on the headrest.

"And one more thing," I mumbled. "We are being followed."

Peter grimaced and looked out the windows. I closed my eyes. Bliss. Bliss. Blissful bliss.

Okay. Where was I going again?

CHAPTER 9
HERE'S DICK CAVETT!

No sooner was I in the ho-ho, gooey-glow from that shot Sad mixed for me, than a nurse sat me down in the lobby of a clinic and gave me even more shots. I guess you really have to be fucked up out of your gourd to get shock treatments.

"Hello Rusty," a dark-skinned, pencil-necked, geek man walked in and sat down next to me. He wore a blue smock. My guess, he was Ethiopian, and not just by the accent.

"Dr. Frankenstein, I presume?"

He smiled. Yeah. Ethiopian.

"Suliman. Dr. Prevell has briefed me on your situation, and I think I may be able to help you?"

"Help me do what?"

"To think better, sir," he said. "Talk better. Feel better. Remember better. Maybe not forever. But we can try."

"If it involves a steady flow of this warm coconut, moo-moo, mix you are shooting me up with, bring it on." I meant it. I liked this stuff. I'd let him stick an umbrella in my head to stay on this beach. The hole was already there.

"Rusty we need for you to sign some papers. This is a tricky procedure…"

"Doc…frankly, it's 11 p.m. and this place looks like the back office of an abortion clinic from the 1960s. It smells tricky here, and it looks tricky here. I would expect nothing less than tricks from you."

"Rusty, we are going to try a series of injections on you also."

"You mean, IN me."

"Yes of course, in you, more precisely."

"Precisely."

"Precisely, in your brain."

Sad now stood in the doorway. Her long arms folded.

"Along with the electric shock treatments, we are going to engage in an experimental process. Do not be alarmed because this is ongoing research in various facilities around the word."

"CIA facilities?" The squirming worm was starting to turn.

"Medical research hospitals and labs," the good Dr. Sad Prevell said.

I looked at her differently now. Did she find a new mad man to stick voodoo needles in? In their brain? My brain? Was that what this trip was all about?

Sad looked at this Dr. Somali-man.

He continued, "We have been injecting brain neurons into test brains. In some cases this injection of brain neurons has improved the thought process of…"

"What, like mice? Monkeys?"

"Yes. Both, in fact."

I looked at my forearms wondering when the automatic metal straps would suddenly appear locking me into the chair.

"The human brain has billions of neurons, all serving a vital part in memory, creativity, focus, intelligence. We inject neurons into the brain in various key locations. You might imagine, sir, with billions there already, how few we might be able to implant with our delivery system…"

"Needles."

"…with each of our needles. The effects are subtle. The results vital. The research vital.

"And working on someone with your obvious brain injury…" Sad said.

"Do you want a lab rat, or do you want to free an innocent man?" I interrupted.

"Both," she answered. "I multi-task."

Well, you know…that was a cool answer. Fast, too.

"The smarter you are, the better you help," she continued.

"Where do you get these needles full of these brain neurons?"

"From the dead. The fresh dead. A variety of people from medical and educational groups have donated their bodies to medical research. A section of them with high IQ's have been parsed to those of us sanctioned and granted to do this research."

I stared at him. Fresh, smart brains on the electric griddle. It did sound interesting.

"Okay. What's a brain needle or two among friends. I have shared way worse."

The nurse put a clipboard on my lap, "Read this and sign here, here, here and here."

My coconut eyes flowed over the papers. I couldn't read a damn thing. I took the pen and signed there, there, there and there.

"We are going to inject you…"

"Whoppeee!"

"…first with some dye and run some tests, some MRIs and then get you into the treatment room. It is best you sleep through as much of the procedure as possible," Doc Franken –brain-stem said.

The nurse rolled up a wheelchair.

"So, we will transfer you into the chair, and…"

"Transfer? Why don't I just sit in it? Save all the ugly transfer fees." I was really unsteady. The chairs were side-by-side. Quaking, I propped myself up and plopped into the narrow wheelchair. I spotted General Grant sitting in a chair down the hall next to Peter the Hulk. I guess there was a ghost waiting room, too. The nurse wheeled me down a long hall for shots and shocks.

"Rusty, do you remember the comedian Dick Cavett?" the nurse asked.

"Yeah."

"Mr. Cavett suffered from depression in the 1980s. He became very disoriented, and Mr. Cavett was given electroshock therapy. He said it was miraculous."

"Miraculous."

"After his treatment, his wife walked into the room, and he sat right up and said, 'Look who's back among the living.' He said it was like a magic wand."

"I'll bet you tell that story to all the head cases."

She laughed, so I must have been funny. And she continued with the medical history lesson as we rolled down one hallway, then another. The hallways were getting darker. Darker and thinner. Dark. Thin. My throat felt like it was submerged in chemicals.

"Rusty, we have administered a very powerful muscle relaxer…"

"I see. I mean I feel. And, I thank you."

"This is because during the shock therapy, we don't want you to hurt your muscles. Your body will…"

"Convulse. Violently. I know. In my prior life I was once an adult. Some people actually break bones during the procedure." The hallways were getting darker still. My stomach felt sick onto itself. It felt like she was tipping the wheelchair over to run it on the two left wheels.

"I don't want you to be afraid."

"Nurse Ratshit, I am afraid to report that I am not afraid."

"Okay," the nurse said.

"Table for five!" I shouted like an idiot. A nice nurse. A sad lawyer. A commando from South Africa. An Ethiopian brain doctor.

"Listen. Hey, we were followed here!" I shouted over my shoulder.

"Peter is looking into it," Sad said from behind.

I started not to care. A mistake. But, I was tanked up on a float-away milkshake. Whew!

"They will kill us!" I shouted and laughed as I said it.

The hallways were darker still! Antiseptic. Pale green tile. Like an old hospital in a horror flick, in a gothic tale, in a nightmare B movie too bloody bad for public television. You get my drift? Then, all the drugs kicked in. Oh man. Dizzy Dean in this rollercoaster chair. Ozzy Osbourne onto the table. I tried to....

I woke up for a few seconds inside a space capsule-like coffin. With that weird MRI marble sound spinning around, cutting me up in sections like a cauliflower. I couldn't even...

Woke up again. Dazed and confused. There was a Rubik's Cube in my mouth. Tasted like rubber, and my breath whistled through a hole in it. I was not at the dentist's office. I was at the electric company. Off in the distance I could hear Doc Frankenstein and the nice nurse, Igor talking. Muffled and like they were 50 miles away. I barely opened one eye. I saw this Doc Frank Salami-man. He looked like he was dressed in butcher-shop clothes and was working over an open oven. A kiln. His foot was pumping some kind of a hearth. Flames licked out the open top. The wind on the hearth was strong, and it whined like people crying. That's right. People crying and moaning. Wailing.

My eyelid closed. I opened it again, but it was like bench

pressing 300 pounds. He had ahold of a long metal rod and held it over the open fire. He looked like a blacksmith in a Western. I think I slept again. Not sure. There were chestnuts roasting on an open fire. Jack Frost...I opened my eye again when the nice nurse started rubbing the sides of my head with a cold, jelly goop. Doc Frank was now wearing cowboy chaps on his legs and a pair of big black frame eyeglasses. He had that blazing rod in his hand. It was red, sizzling hot! He came closer to me. That thing was crackling hot. Cooking the air.

"Now all I have to do is insert this white-hot rod through his temples," he said.

He said that? What? No! Nooooooo! No! NOOOOOOOOOO!

He did it! He put the rod through my head! He stabbed my head! He put it right through my head! "Noooo! NOOOOO!"

"Ten seconds."

My body left the table. I was exorcised! I mean it went up off the table, and my body rolled in the air like a tidal wave. Power rays shot off the tips of my fingers. Every cell in body was nuked up!

"Five seconds."

That's all of that I remember. I passed out again from the hot pipe in my head, or the drugs. Or both. Maybe I died.

******

I opened both my eyes. I was frozen in pain. Every muscle, and I mean every muscle down to my toes, ached. It hurt to breathe. It hurt to think. Pumping blood hurt. Two heads came into view. The nice nurse and the hot rod doc.

"How are you feeling, Rusty."

"You know, I am a drug addict?" I mumbled.

"Ahhh, no," the nurse said.

"When you want to drug me, you have to up the dose

because I take a lot of drugs. You have to really drug me."

They just stared at me.

"I woke up during the ignition and blast off."

"Oh my."

"I woke up."

"We are very sorry," the doc said.

They dabbed at my eye corners, my nose and mouth. No doubt I was leaking my rusty blood from these torn apart holes.

Sad's face came into view.

"How did it go?" she asked.

"You are a sight for sore eyes."

"Thank you."

"No. Even my eyes are sore."

"This type of treatment is similar to having a grand mal seizure," Sad said. "Every bit of you will be very sore. As though you ran a 50-mile marathon, I am told."

I grunted. Every bit of me was sore. They undid the straps on my arms and legs. They put hands on my shoulder blades and lifted my torso up. Ohhh, God! I have never in my life been this deeply and thoroughly sore. Ever. Everywhere. How thorough could this be?

I sat up, looked around. A clock on a table read 5:30 a.m. in the morning. I saw the black rubber block they inserted in my mouth laying on a metal tray. General Grant was standing by the door, looking at me all concerned, puffing on his cigar.

"Can he smoke in here?" I babbled.

"Do you still see the General?" Sad asked.

"Yes. Am I not supposed to?"

"No."

"Hey," I said to the General, "guess whose back with the living…dead?"

Grant nodded at me.

What? You were expecting maybe…Dick Cavett?

CHAPTER 10
QUASI-PEACEFUL OVERLOAD

Two p.m. I stood near the window. Two stories up. Trees and the Hudson River. Upriver. Upstate. A far cry from the river view by the city under the George Washington Bridge, the spot down the river where I met Alphonso the Crepe Hanger just three days ago. Two days? I was now in hospital pajamas, but this was not a hospital, it was Dr. Suliman's clinic for the mentally disturbed, deranged and therefore subsequent brain fried. When I was a teenager I climbed up, then down, Bear Mountain, not too far from here, which wasn't like scaling Kilimanjaro, but that night and for the next three days my muscles ached as if it were. This muscle ache was way worse. Even my scruffy, un-shaven beard hairs hurt.

Someone knocked on the door, and the nurse walked in. She was tall. I never saw her while I was standing to gauge her height. Nurse Helen Marchant was on a metallic name tag. She set a tray down.

"Miss Marchant, I feel as though I was run over by a

steamroller."

"You must, Rusty. Here are some pain pills. Are you hungry?"

I swallowed the two horse pills. I gulped the water. I could not remember the last time I drank a glass of water. It tasted great.

"What's on this menu?" I asked softy, sitting down on the bed in slow-motion.

"Soup and sandwich."

"And more of that water, please. The whole barrel sounds good."

It looked like a king's meal. I bit into the toasted ham and cheese half and caught every flavor. Felt the crunch of the toast, the softness of the ham and the cheese.

"I must be more than hungry."

She smiled at me.

"In an hour, Dr. Prevell and Dr. Suliman will be in with some results from your tests and your treatment. How does your head feel?"

"Uncomfortably numb," I mumbled with my mouth full. I sipped the soup. It was chicken soup. My ex-wife, Nancy, has a book called Chicken Soup for the Soul. I suddenly remembered holding it in my hands. Leafing through the pages with my thumb. I could see her face and hear her explaining to me what it meant. I caught a piece of chicken with my spoon and ate it.

"You are an amazing cook, or I am a starving POW."

She left. Returned with a pitcher of water. I finished the meal. I leaned back against the pillows of the bed. While I looked out the window, I drank several glasses of the delicious water. The pills fought back some of the pain. I was still numb, but two words came to my mind about laying there then. Quasi-peaceful overload. Is that three words? It was a mouthful like those pills were.

Within the hour, Sad, Suliman and Peter walked into my room.

"Rusty," Sad said.

"Doctor. Doctor. Hulk."

They were carrying oversized files and x-rays.

"First things first," I said. "What have you done about the people following us last night?"

"They were police," Peter said. "Plainclothes in an unmarked car."

"They must be outside now. Outside watching somehow."

"They are," Peter said.

"Police such as they are," Sad said, "We cannot take action on them. Anything we do…"

"…would be an assault on a police officer. Interfering. No, I guess not. They are afraid you will treat me and maybe fix me," I said.

"About that…" Sad said. The music in her voice was not good. The way she said – "about that."

"We'll lose them when we leave. They will follow the limo. We won't be in it. Yes, and about that, 'about that'," I said.

Dr. Suliman sat on the end of my bed and opened some files.

"Rusty, you have some serious brain damage that will never completely heal."

He started to slide some medical scans and photos across the bed to me. I waved them off.

"Skip the pics, Doc. I can't read 'em. All those look like x-rays of a vegetable salad to me. I know that my brains are scrambled. Good eggs mixed with bad eggs. I am not in this for me. For…the cure. There is no cure. I came to you, Sad, to get this mess with Steverino cleared up."

"Dr Suliman and I have worked together for years in Africa," Sad said. "We have been pioneering efforts in DNA research and brain injury. What we could do in

Africa, we cannot do, or even treat with our methods in the United States."

"What has this got to do with Steverino?"

"Everything. We need you at your very best. I want to show you something." She pulled out a plastic pull bottle and rattled it. "We have been working on and testing a medication for years in Africa. A brain stimulus. Memory is largely chemical, Rusty. The brain is a road map. This pill is like a rainstorm, a flood, that …that flows over the existing roads and floods to other roads as well, making them stronger."

I looked into the crappy plastic bottle at the horse pills inside.

"The floods cross over to roads that were never connected before and those that were connected before but aren't connected now."

"And the shock treatment?"

"We have learned through studies that the pills work best after shock treatments. The shock seems to create the thunderstorm that causes the rain…"

"…that causes the floods." I nodded. "And that…is the Sesame Street explanation of your pill. Rain and floods and roads." I could get that.

They both nodded. Peter the Hulk just stared at me. I don't think he liked me.

"And I thought I was in a medical clinic, not the weather center. So am I an agent of justice or a lab rat?"

"Both," Sad said. "When you came into my lobby? When I found out who you were? I would have done both things separately; taken you here for my tests and helped you to free an innocent man. I have many comrades in the legal system that work with me. Overtly, or covertly. I called one in the District Attorney's Office, and he said you were once a brilliant and effective detective. And you were an honest and good man."

Ohhh now, that hurt. That suddenly hurt me in my chest. Like someone died kind of, like it hurt my heart, you know? They said, honest. Good. Brilliant. Effective. My right eye got watery. I know why, but I don't know why. Being all those things is quite a responsibility. I can't do all that thinking. I can't live up to that.

"Who said that?"

"The district attorney himself."

"Oh. Him. What is this medication called, Comrade Sad?" I said with a snort up my right nostril to get a handle on the drainage. My nose always got wet from tears in my eyes. I should say "eye," because my left eye was dry. Right eye-cry. Left eye dry. Maybe I am a visual schizophrenic?

"We call it Zulu."

"Zulu!"

"It stands for something. Zumeric, Ulmat…"

"Stop!" I told her. "I don't want to know. I thought it might stand for 'tall black men sticking spears in my head.' Hey, why not? It seems to be a hot target for everyone. Mafia. Cops. And now Thor, the God of Thunder here. Why not savannah tribesman?"

Sad leaned forward and looked into my eyes with a small flashlight. I let her. At this point I'd let her put me in the electric chair.

"You are making a little more sense now. Looking better…" she whispered, intent on my eyeballs… "Rusty. Track my finger. You are showing your master's degree in world history from Columbia University?"

"Go Lions," I whispered, "and my keen sense of Nordic Gods from Marvel Comics."

"Got game, lion?" she asked as she opened the pill bottle and took out a big Zulu for little old me.

"Gimme, said the lab rat to the black widow, spider woman." I opened my mouth, and she inserted the pill into it. She got my glass of water and handed it to me.

"What's another addiction?" I said.

"You told us you were an addict last night," Dr. Suliman said. "What drugs?"

"Anything and everything."

"Ever try to quit? Ever have any withdrawal?"

"Never tried to quit. Never had to. I have quit some things and started others. Never had any kind of withdrawal like my friends." ...were they friends? Yeah, some were.

"Rusty, I don't think you have many addiction centers still left working in your brain," he said.

What do you say to that? Oh, I thought of something clever–

"New meaning to the words non habit-forming."

"The human brain is as mysterious as the universe," Doc Salami said.

Okay, Carl Sagan.

We all just sat around or stood in silence after that one, for a few seconds.

"You take a nap," Sad said. "We will get out of here at 6 p.m...."

"Not in the limo. That's a decoy."

"Right. We'll have another car. We can pull it in around back, out of their sight. We are going to see a DEA agent tonight that I know very well in Staten Island."

"We need everything on Delafasio."

"He will get that for us. Sleep now."

"Sleep."

They started to leave, then Sad turned to me and added, "Rusty, your eyes are blinking in synch today."

"Now, if I could only pee and shit at the same time."

"Don't press your luck, Tarzan," she said.

"See. I am not completely healed, and I still have impulsive, Tourette's-like idiosyncrasies."

Which is why I said that in the first place. I too can

be shocking in a shock treatment facility. And who wants to be all healed up and be that honest and good and effective man? Sounds like a lot of damn work to me. And boring, too. No thanks.

Me and the Zulu tablet laid back on the bed. Wonder where General Grant was this afternoon? Would he soon be replaced by Shaka Zula? I'd settle for Chaka. Chaka Khan. Chaka Khan. Chaka Khan. Oh yeah, cops are outside in a car down the street waiting to shoot me.

Where were we going again tonight?

CHAPTER 11
THE FLAMING MATCHSTICK

Black. Black turtleneck. Black leather jacket. Black pants. Black shoes and socks. Red hair. I look like a rap club's custom-made, matchstick. Outfit by Peter and his trip to the local mall. I stood near a window in the dark lobby and peered through sheer curtains to watch the undercover police car parked down the street. It was raining. Sunset.

They were still watching us. Watching for me. I guess they knew I'd run to Sad's foundation for help? Maybe a mole snitch in the Foundation, too? Last week I would have gotten a screwdriver from the basement, hopped some backyard fences, crawled up to their car, sneaked into their backseat and shoved the screwdriver into the backs of their Five Ape brains. Medulla Oblongata their ass with a flathead or phillips. Spread the head holes all up and around this joint. Why should I be the only one whistling in the wind?

But I was too weak-kneed and weak-brained for it now. Hurts me just to stand here and breathe. All Zulu-ed up. A thunderstorm in my brain made me…is sensible a word? Sensible. How do you spell it? It wasn't s-e-n-s-i-b-l-e to stab them with screwdrivers. They were cops, ostensibly working a surveillance s-t-a-k-e-o-u-t. It would be insensible to bring down the wrath of One Police Plaza upon Sad and Peter. And me. Me, too. Me, the flaming matchstick. Not while Steverino depended upon us.

I have so many secrets from Sad. Things I can never, ever tell her. Tell anyone. My life has been ruined by the things I have done. Things with screwdrivers and knives and guns.

Outside the limo drove down the mostly residential street of the Suliman clinic and made the harsh, sudden turn into this driveway below. Down the street in the sedan, I saw their little beady ape heads bounce into life. The limo pulled around the back of the building out of their sight. I heard some voices and the opening and shutting of some car doors. Then the limo left but did not drive back past the super sleuths. I heard the police engine turn on, and they gunned their car after the limo. Punked!

"Rusty!" I heard Peter shout from downstairs.

Every step was a wince and a pain, but yours truly persevered and got down the back stairs and out into the back lot. I saw the getaway car. A dark maroon sedan. Peter was behind the wheel, Sad in the front passenger seat. I lowered myself into the open back seat of the car. It was a challenge, and, at first, I thought I couldn't do it. I felt like a burn victim that was also hit by a garbage truck that was also struck by lightning. It's the ultimate workout. Multiple seizures. Who needs a treadmill? PX-Seizure.

"Hi, I'm Rusty, and I have got the exercise program for you. Just let me shoot you in the head in just the right place that only I can do. I know where it is, and that is what you pay me for. Then I'll jam some lightning bolts right down the hole with a special mixture of brain amoebas only

African scientists have deciphered. Then it will all go to work on you. Every day, get a fantastic workout! You'll pass out, miss and forget about the hardest workout of your life. A seizure! You'll wake up on the road each day to a fantastic body even movie stars wished they had."

"Pain pills," Sad said, handing me two tablets over her shoulder, snapping me out of my commercial plans.

I took them and chomped them down as Peter pulled the sedan out onto the street. She handed me a large carry-out cup from a fast food joint. I sucked on the straw, and it was a strawberry milkshake. God it was great. What a fabulous array of creamy flavor! It coated my dry, achy throat. I wanted to take a bath in the stuff.

"We are going to see that comrade in Staten Island. He will help us do the research we need," she said. "He has been assigned to a federal narcotics task force and has access to a phenomenal amount of information. He has helped us clear people on death row before."

"Onward Christian cooomrades," I sang. I slurped. I sang. I slurped. I sang. I sang some more. I slurped.

Sad started in on her cell phone, yacking to people about court cases for nearly an hour. Finally, she put the phone down in her lap and sighed a sigh of frustration. She shook her head.

"Lots of trouble with lots of cases?" I asked.

"Lots," she answered. "I have five people on death rows in three states I am working on, and 23 in jail on other felonies that I think DNA will clear if we can persuade the systems to even test it all."

"Sad…I have a secret about my wife," I blurted out. I don't know why. I just blurted it out.

"You do? Would you like to share that secret? With Peter and me?"

"My wife Nancy …my ex-wife is not her. She is an

actress or something. A plant. She is not my wife. She is a substitute woman." It came out in a flurry.

Sad turned to look back at me and hung a long thin arm over the back of her seat.

"A substitute?"

I told her everything. How when I woke from the coma, my wife was an actress. But she could be heard in another room. Or on the phone.

"I don't understand why she would do this to me. How could she arrange this? Why? And spy on me?"

"Rusty we have to do a battery of tests on you yet. There are many things we need to ascertain and document about you and your brain damage."

"You think it's me? This is too elaborate to be a dream or a hallucination."

"When this man, who shot you years ago, informed you about Steverino the other night? Something happened to you that night. You were healing in some way, and then this news had a deep effect on you, your brain and your brain's healing process. Something is working itself…out. Re-connecting. Working together and making you take action."

"Makes me feel sick. Weird."

"Understandable. This is very uncomfortable. I would presume that you have had periods of these weird uncomfortable sick times in the past? As your brain tries to heal itself."

"I have. Yes. But that doesn't explain why my wife hired someone to pretend to be her yet hung around to watch it all."

"Rusty, there a syndrome called Capgras. Ever hear of it?"

"No."

"It's rare and I wouldn't suppose that you had it without testing. But, people who have had brain injuries, in some rare cases, report that they are unable to recognize, say, one of their parents. Or their spouse. They function completely in every way in their world, perfectly normal, but for this one thing. They cannot identify a certain person that was once important to them. There is a case on record where a man could not identify his poodle."

"But she is really there. I heard her talking out in the halls, or on the phone."

"Rusty, with Capgras, your visual path of recognition was damaged, but not your audio path. Your hearing still works. Visually, no. There is glitch. You can recognize the voice, but you cannot recognize her image. The image interferes with the audio. You can only recognize her when you can't see her."

"I…don't understand."

"People with Capgras cannot comprehend Capgras. From what you have told me already, you may have a classic case of it."

Well, I was blown away over that. How could I not recognize my own wife? Impossible. I became frightened. I tumbled into my own mind. I moaned slightly. My breath got short. I really want to figure this out…

"RUSTY!"

She was calling me.

"Rusty, when we get the chance, Dr. Suliman and I will give you a thorough testing of your brain."

"Hmmmp! Dr. Salami-Man? He is not the same guy I saw last night. Two doctors."

"Two…doctors?"

"The Dr. Suliman I saw this morning is not the same doctor I saw talking to me in the lobby last night. Not the same doctor giving me the shock treatments, and not the same doctor who came in with you this morning."

"Three doctors."

"Yeah, three then. Three Sulimans. They are not the same person."

"They are, Rusty. I mean, he is," she said.

"We're here," Peter said.

Sad's gaze lingered on me like I'd just crept right off this Mister Capgras chart. "We'll talk about this later." We left the car and walked to a side entrance door of a bland government building.

How many police stations have I been in? City. County. State. Federal. Jails. How many? This one was a state substation in Staten Island. We stood by the back door, and Peter rang a buzzer. I felt almost comfortable in this chilly hall waiting to enter yet another door of yet another police building. I saw the figure of a man walk down a dark hall toward us. He threw a few locks and pushed open the door.

"Come on in."

We all followed him back down this hall and deeper into the building. I saw all the signs on the doors for commander this-and-that, and room this-and-that. Bulletin boards with cop admin shit on it. The deeper I walked, the deeper I felt at home. But, an antiseptic home. It isn't home. It's a way station. The antiseptic flavor of a place you love and hate, a structure built to facilitate, to pass people through and through and through. Hire. Replace. Fire. Promote. You know. Cop home. Move along. Nothing to see here but wrecked health, wrecked marriages, frustration and a millennium of boredom interrupted with explosions of life and death insta-seconds. You leave? The hull remains. Like a bullet casing.

We filed into an office with computers. Some looked old. Some looked new.

"Stanley, this is Rusty," Sad said. "You know Peter."

"Hi," Stanley said.

Peter nodded to him.

Who names their kid Stanley? This guy was about 30 years old. The era of Stanleys died long before that.

"Comrade Stanley, got any coffee?" I asked.

"Nah, not right near. Across the building by the night shift. But I gotta tell ya, I'd rather not have anybody see youse guys are in here." He shrugged his shoulders. He was a small guy. Curly brown hair. Big nose. Dressed in Dockers. I mean fully. Dockers pants. Dockers shirt. I don't know about the belt. Dockers shoes.

"Marion Delafasio," Stanley the Docker cop said. "I got started on him. Looked him up and looked up this China Doll murder." He handed Sad a folder. "Normal looking guy. Normal background. Works middle-management in a clothing factory in New Yawk."

I smiled at Sad and slipped the folder from her crossed arms. I sat at a desk, switched on a lamp and opened the file.

"As youse can see, no criminal history."

"Is he still the next-door neighbor of that Chinese diplomat?" I asked. "Has he moved?"

"He has not moved, but the diplomat, Mr. Bo Zoup has moved."

"Where?"

Dockers turned to his computer. Typed. I scanned the other files. About ten pages. Shallow.

"Bo Zoup. The guy moved back to China," he said.

"Shit!" I said. "We need to know where in China." I stood, handed Sad the folder back and leaned on a desk by Dockers. "That a nice surface-scratcher file on Delafasio. Now let's get busy. I want finances. Back finances. Crime time finances. And right after the crime finances. His. His wife. Father. Mother. Brother. Sister. Dog. CARS. Boats. Motorcycles. Everything attached to a penny. This was a setup and a setup is usually with money. Gifts. Get me credit cards."

Dockers looked at Sad. Sad looked sad.

"I know you need a warrant for all this," I said. "But we

have no probable cause. We're looking for probable cause."

"Fishing expedition," Sad mumbled, sadly.

"Oh yeah. We're fishing. And you can't catch any fish if you don't go on an expedition. Play magic fingers!" I waved my fingers at him, in the air.

Even Peter the Hulk nodded at Sad.

Dockers started in zipping around in the illegal access world of the internet.

"You want this back?" she asked me about the file.

"Nope. Memorized." I wasn't kidding. I took my heady snapshots of each page. Kerplunk.

"Looks like Mr. Delafasio bought a new Cadillac one week after the Downing conviction."

"Caddy. Bought or was given?"

"Well, he had a new one registered in his name."

"BOUGHT or GIVEN?"

Docker typing.

"No finances on that. No car loan. Just got a Caddy."

"Run the VIN Number. Track it. From where. Track. Track. Track. Track."

Docker typing. And I smelled blood.

"Chesterfield Cadillac in Passaic, New Joysey."

"Jersey. Salesman. Get me the salesman."

Docker typing. Typing.

"Vincent Linkos. Salesman. Chesterfield Cadillac. Cash deal, I guess. No loan."

"Cash deal. Now, Mr. Investigator Stanley with the magic fingers, at that time, around that time, who else got a Cadillac from Vincent Linkos? Especially the same kind of Cadillac. Especially a resident not in New Jersey. Cash, please for starters."

Typing. Where was that coffee again?

Julian Managos. Vermont."

"Loan?"

"No, must have been cash. I see no loan paperwork. Filed the same day."

"And there Sad, is the secret, confidential informant who tipped off the locals about where the China Doll was buried in Vermont. Julian Managos. He called Crime Stoppers. Lied about seeing a suspect described as Steverino Downing dumping a body. Gave them Steverino's license plate."

Sad was trying to take it all in. Peter nodded his head up and down and, for the first time in days, the Dutch Boer brute was even smiling.

"Make sure there are no loans on those cars. See if all other Linkos sales are with loans. Any other cash deals?"

Then, I turned to Sad and Peter. "It's a touch. A Mafia touch. A Five Apes touch. The gift of a car, like a Caddy, or whatever. An arrangement. A payoff. They use the same car salesman, one they trust, and their people get gifts of cars and whatever else. The car is an added bonus."

"There are no other cash deals for his other sales. All are with loans. Different days."

"Okay."

"And this Managos guy is a dirt bag."

Stanley typed.

We gathered around the screen and took a look at his face and rap sheet. A few arrests for drugs. Loan sharking. Agg assault. Gun charge. Hell, nothing I ain't already done or way worse in the last few years. And then and there I felt badly about that. Jesus, I hope I wouldn't start to cry again, you know? What was the difference between that dirt bag on the screen and the red headed dirt bag in the reflection of the screen? Me? Oh, my God, I felt badly. Badly, badly, badly, badly, badly, badly. Our faces appeared to melt into the screen. What was I once? What had I become? There are so many secrets Sad cannot know. I stood up and looked at her. I was a hider. A hider of ugly secrets. A wolf man looking at the full moon. Dracula at night. Rusty blood stains in my armpits. Under my jacket. Can she see through me?

"He once had stock in an ice cream company," Stanley found.

"Details," I demanded.

Docker typing.

"In 2001 he owned stock in the Brattleboro Ice Creamery."

"Still?"

"No. Sold it in 2004."

"Any other stocks?"

"No."

"Hmm," I hummed.

"Ice cream?" Sad asked.

I sat on the corner of a desk and explained, "In the late 1990s, the Boston Mob got very interested in ice cream. They kept hearing about the success of *Ben & Jerry's Ice Cream* in Vermont. It was a very successful business with national shipping and distribution. And run by, you know, two hippies. Boston wanted in on this. The Mob bought up some Vermont and New Hampshire ice cream companies. Probably Brattleboro is one. And they started squeezing *Ben & Jerry* every way they could. Shit got serious. They stole some recipes. Messed with drivers. Burned some buildings. Couple of people got killed. The Feds called this the Ice Cream Wars."

"Ice Cream Wars?" Peter repeated.

"Yeah. Anytime you can run refrigerated trucks all over the U.S. and into Canada, you can run all kinds of bodies, guns, drugs, stolen property. And you can sell expensive ice cream, too! And when the goods are perishable, easily perishable like milk or ice cream, you have waste. You have great write-offs to invent. It's a great company for laundering and hiding money."

They were all staring at me like I was crazy. Or worse, like I wasn't crazy.

"Peter and I will visit this Vincent the car dealer," I said.

"Won't he tip the Apes off? The Mob?" Sad asked.

"Not the way I visit. He won't want to tip anybody off. Stanley, can you get us anything on the Ice Cream Wars? Can you get any connection to this guy and the Boston Mob?"

Stanley stood and spoke with Sad. I leaned into the screen and took a mental snapshot of the criminal history and face. Kerplunk it went into the fold, the crevice, that brain wrinkle that keeps all that straight. I stared at the face. I also saw the big red-topped "it" in the reflection on the screen. Me. Another mind pit I can't seem to grasp, to understand.

CHAPTER 12
A SKINNED GHOST

"You can't come with me, Peter," I told him as we watched the car dealer's daughter back out of the house garage. We were lucky enough to see the front and back of his house through the trees from where we were parked. The northeast Jersey home was on a rural, hilly street.

"I can't let you go alone, Sad said…"

"Peter, you are a respectable guy. You have a private investigator's license in the State of New York. You look like an action movie star, and you talk funny. You cannot be seen. You cannot be identified."

"For a crazy man, you can make a lot of sense. What are you going to do?"

"Nothing that tips the cops, the Mob and the Apes off. We need them dumb."

"I am…I have to trust you."

"And I am going to trust you trusting me. When I work with partners…well…" What was I about to say anyway? Something goofy? Corny? Old Rusty-doodle had a true–

blue, partner-trust line for that moment, but I didn't find it in the Rusty archives. Must be in a filing cabinet that was shot out.

Just then the wife left the house. She left in a nice Caddy of course. I had ten minutes to get across the vacant lots and near the garage door, if he followed the same pattern as the last two days.

"Toodles," I said, and left the car.

Jeez. Why did I say toodles? What a stupid word and stupid thing to say. Toodles, for Christ sakes. Because, I was thinking about Rusty-doodles? Man! Peter's gonna think I am a faggot or something to say...toodles.

I got to the corner of the house. And waited. The garage door was still open, and one more big sedan remained inside. Vincent's place. Nice, big, open yard. Trees. People have no idea how nice New Jersey can be when you drive 20 minutes out of the big cities. A person could – ohhh! The house door. Vincent Linkos was going to work. Or so he thought.

I stepped into the large garage. I smiled, because this was going to be some fun like I sometimes like to have. Hey, everyone needs a hobby.

Vincent raised his bushy eyebrows at the sight of me and pursed his purple lips to say a word that started with a "W..."

I quickly helped him out with some "W" words because his "W" was not working out for him. I said for him, "Who are you? What the fuck are you doing in my garage? What do you want? Where did you get those shoes? What manly cologne is that? Or just like...WHAT the fuck?"

"Who are you?" he completed his own sentence! Which in meaning, included all the above except for the shoes and cologne. I'd like to think that I helped.

"I share my name with a skinless ghost," I said as I marched up to him. Before he could step back, I grabbed two handfuls of his overcoat and shoved him about five feet. He almost fell over. There was a big plush couch up against the garage back wall.

"Sit."

He sat on the arm of the couch, his face chock full of fright. Fear - this was like a double expresso to yours truly.

"If you want something? I've got …what…what do you want? I've got some money. There's a big screen TV…"

I looked up on the wall, and sure enough I saw the big screen TV. In a garage? Then I understood the couch.

"I need the name or names of mobsters who buy cars with cash from you, Vincent."

"Huh…what…does someone owe somebody money? I don't. What? I mean…they buy the cars…I mean."

"The name or names."

"Are you collecting some money? What? I don't owe them money. What is this all about? I can't tell you anything. Do you work with them?" he asked, frantically.

"I am not with them, Vincent. But, you know how Mob guys act. These guys that collect money and they rough people up, bounce them around? But they lie. They lie to you because they really aren't there to collect money. They are really there to rough you up. They really like roughing people up, otherwise they wouldn't do it. They lie. They are liars, Vinnie. They like to hide behind the lines, 'nothing personal.' And it's just business.' No. It's about the pain. In their pants they got a hard on when you break a sweat or turn pale, or when they see a little blood."

I leaned on the work bench. "Me? I am not a liar. I am not, really, really not here to get a name from you. Not really. Deep down, I am in this for the terror. The sheeeeer terror. The terror in your eyes. The terror in your blood vessels as your fat fuck heart beats out of your chest. But…I also need the names? The names are secondary, Vinnie. Secondary to the terror."

He was as mesmerized as he was confused. Hence fore, I continued…

"You sit at your desk or in the back seat of a Cadillac on test drives, you fat fuck, selling cars, as all kinds of fat corpuscles swarm around your heart and gut and neck like worms digging holes out of your life every day, you fat fuck. You know what your epitaph is gonna be? Huh? You know what an epitaph is? It's what your life meant. Your…tombstone, Vincent. Here was. Here lies. Here lies Big Vinnie. A little worm of the Mob. Digging the guts outta life every day. And for that…what…you get more car sales? Pocket money? A TV in your garage? That watch? Take off that watch, Vinnie…"

"You can have the watch…"

"I don't want the watch. Take it off."

He did and held it up for me. It was a gold-colored watch. I don't know watch names, but it must have been a good one, don't you think? It looked more like a lady's watch to me. Thin. Fancy. Leather strap.

"Eat it Vinnie."

"Wha?"

"Eat it. Eat it like spaghetti. Like you swallow chicken. Like you eat big steaks! EAT IT!"

Vincent put it to his lips and stopped. His eyes watered. His face looked shocked. That was the terror I was looking for.

"EAT IT!"

Gagging, sobbing, he held the watch with his mouth slightly open. I leaned over and grabbed his chin and shoved it closed.

"Swallow. SWALLOW!"

He did. Oh boy. He coughed. He gagged, he choked, but somehow it when down the pipes. I let him go.

"A guy like you really can't enjoy something unless you can fuck it or eat it. Right, Vinnie? Right? Consume.

Consume it. Now THAT is consumption. When you shit it out later? Rinse it off. Then you have your pretty watch back. And then you can really enjoy it. Because you have finally, really consumed it. You are a consumer. The consummate consumer. Put it back on your wrist and show car consumers how rich you are with your special watch. You will have finally consummated your relationship with a wealthy object."

The guy was now fucked up. His head shook, and he gasped each time the watch dropped another inch on its way down to his stomach.

"Aggghhhh!" he cried out. Then gasped. He touched his chest. "Aaahhhh, Aggghhhh!"

"The names of the guys who bought the cars to give to Delafasio in New York and Managos in Vermont."

"They will kill me…."

"They will never know. Why? Because I don't want them tipped off. I just want to know. It's your secret right here with only me the skinless ghost."

"You don't know who you are dealing with!"

"Dealing? Dealing implies that I am playing a game with them. Dealing implies I exist in their casino of life. Dealing implies I sit at their table and receive the cards. Receive the dice. Vincent, dealing means that I accept some kind of…rules. Rules? Like house rules, ya know?" I walked a few steps away and rested a hand back on his garage bench. "Do I look like someone who plays by house rules? What does your gut instinct think about that? Your time-bomb ticking gut?"

"You know they are going to have to cut this watch out of my stomach."

"Do tell?"

"What, what will I tell them? What will I tell my wife? I have a watch in my stomach."

"I know Vinnie. Tell them…tell them that you were…
you know…checking the time and you brought your watch
up to your fat face…and…oops…you accidentally swallowed your watch with your fat mouth! Yeah. Tell them
that. Or first, give it a day. Eat some grains and some fiber,
a couple of dried prunes and, who knows? Maybe gravity
will win the day." You know, I thought that was funny. I
laughed a bit, because, well, you have to admit that is a
little funny, right?

"The names, Vincent. Or that pretty watch will not be
the only thing in your stomach. I will make you eat every
fucking thing on this work bench here, and some of this
stuff here …look at it…it's pretty fucking big stuff. A lot
of sharp ends, too. How tough are your teeth?"

He sighed.

I picked up a glass jar of small nails.

"Ralph Ponzone and Jackie G."

I nodded. I sat down on the other arm of the couch.

"Jackie G."

"Yes," he whimpered.

"Big guy. Big fedora. Too big a brim?" I asked.

"Yeah," He groaned.

"Big face, big neck. Face like a raw egg? Pale. Like he
shaved way too close? Like purple veins and red lines and
spots all over his face."

"Yeah."

Jackie G. I knew him. Jackie Galardo. NYPD Captain.
Works at the Plaza. Five Apes. Ponzone was WOP Mafia.
I took a deep breath and sized up the garage.

"You have this big beautiful house, and you must come
out here and, what - lay on this couch and watch football
games on Sundays? Right here in the garage?"

"Baseball, too," he said.

"Mets? Yankees?"

"Both."

I nodded. "Yeah, I can see that. Right out here with a breeze and the trees blowing in the background. What is the deal you have with these guys?" I asked.

"They come out to the dealership and pay cash for Cadillacs. I guess for people who help them out. People they owe favors to. They tell me who gets them, and these people either come in and pick up the keys, or we deliver the cars. I sell them about eight to 10 cars a year this way."

"Hmmm. You remember all the car sales to these special guys?"

"Oh yeah. I know who these guys are, and I know something is up when they come in and buy cars. They could be buying cars for hit men. I don't know. They make me nervous. But they act like perfect gentlemen. They have to come see me direct."

"You remember these customers? Delafasio and Managos? Years ago."

"Yeah."

"How did this go exactly?"

"Delafasio drove out here from the city and got his car."

"Who drove him to the dealership?"

"Must have been his wife? I dunno. Some woman about his age. She was all bubbly."

"Bubbly."

"Yeah."

"New Cadillac bubbly," I guessed.

He nodded.

"That watch hurting you down there yet?" I pointed to his stomach.

"Not yet."

"The other guy in Vermont? Managos."

"One of our shop guys drove it up there."

We stared at each other.

"I get a good commission. I get more sales for the month. The year. Sales."

"Sales. I understand."

"How did you find me?"

"Vincent, there is a paper trail. Buyers. Sellers. Financing, or no financing. Salesmen. You yourself did nothing wrong. You just sold some cars. But it's to the Mob. And to really dirty cops. You knew it was the Mob. And anytime you do anything with the Mob, anytime you touch the Mob, you breathe in the air around them... you smell their perfume. It's dangerous, Vinnie. Very dangerous. Anything. Anytime. I don't have to tell you that now. I will not tell them I was here. I will not do that to you. I don't want them to know."

I stood up.

"Are you a cop? A private eye?"

"None of those things. And because I am none of those things? I will win."

"Win what?"

"A very temporary stay of execution in the never-ending battle of good versus evil."

"And you are...a good guy?"

"No. But if I come in for a Cadillac someday, it's safe to sell me one."

"What will I do when they come back? Should I sell them more cars?"

"Probably. You can't let them know about this. You have to keep selling to them. Because...you're in. When you're in, you're in. Here's the deal. If they smell shit on your watch? They'll kill ya. Some morning when...when your wife and daughter leave the house, they'll catch you right in this garage like I did. But they won't make you eat jewelry and nails and shit. They'll kill ya."

"You part of a Mob? You can't be a cop."

"I'm a part of nothing, Vinnie. I don't know what to tell you about that watch. Give it day or two then see a doctor, huh?"

"Yeah."

"So long."

"So long."

I walked out of the garage and across the back yard and turned through the field along the tree line back to Peter's car. Ralph Ponzone and Captain Jack Galardo. I knew them. I remembered them. Middle management. Made men in their worlds. Two puppets in a charade to kill an innocent Chinese woman, to scare her Chinese diplomat husband into smuggling drugs into the USA. She's dead and the patsy Steverino is next.

Out on the road I heard some kids. I looked over to the house across from Vincent's. Two kids, off to school, telling their mom goodbye. Another day in the life. Another morning. The mom waved as the dad and kids drove off to everyday work and everyday school. Everyday life-land.

Toodles. Yeah, toodles is how my kids said goodbye to us in the morning. To me and my real wife Nancy - not that imposter bitch. Toodles! The whole of this neighborhood was toodles. When I got through with all this? Gonna question this imposter and get to the bottom of all her lies. Yeah! Bitch.

CHAPTER 13
GET A GUN. LOAD IT.

I knew what I had to do.

I was on the hotel treadmill in their fitness room. The lights were bright and I looked very, very pale just walking on the treadmill. Just walking. The TV news was on, and a New York Congressman had just confessed to sending pictures of his wiener to women he didn't know on the internet. I remember this guy from when I worked organized crime. Clean as a whistle. No Mob connections. Ideologue. But his bubble squeezed out and burst in other directions. Everybody's got a bubble, or a tumor.

"Hey Rusty!" My bodyguard shouted from the door. "Holy Mother of God, Rusty you have been freakin' walking on dat thing for three hours. It's 11:15, p.m. huh? Let's go up and get to bed."

My bodyguard was not happy. Three hours? Was I walking for three hours? I bet I burned at least 11 calories.

"Yeah, yeah," I told the guy. My shadow. Peter's night shift guy. I was shadowed around the clock. Sad's orders.

Put in this Hilton in Jersey like a hot house tomato. Nice digs. She said she was working some legal angles for Steverino, but I know it ain't going to work out. I know what I have to do, and I can't be shadowed to do it.

I stepped off the machine and shut it down. Grabbed the towel.

"Let's go Lamont," I said, walking to the door.

"Lamont?"

"As in Lamont Cranston, not Lamont Sanford."

"Don't know either of them."

"Well, Lamont Cranston is the Shadow. Lamont Sanford is Redd Foxx's TV son."

"Oh."

"Sanford and Son?"

"Oh."

"Oh." Where did this zoob grow up? I got to do what I got to do alone. I need a gun and a car and a credit card. Got the clothes.

"You can walk for three hours like dat?" he asked me as we strolled to the elevator.

"I was shot right in the head. I can do a lot of things I couldn't do before. I can't do a lot of things I could do before."

He smiled and nodded.

******

The elevator door closed behind us. I wanted to hit him on the throat and take his car keys, wallet and that pussy little pistol he was wearing, and do what I gotta do. I stared at his profile.

"What?" He noticed my glaring.

"Nothing." I would wait to speak with Sad first thing tomorrow morning. She was coming for me. I would wait.

Floor 2. Floor 3. Floor 4. Lamont's Adam's apple was

just sticking right out waiting for the edge of my hand to collapse. It was mine like a vampire. I gasped.

"WHAT?" He noted my gasp.

"See, I am out of breath after three hours of walking." I took some deep breaths. No act. I was trying not to kill Lamont. Tomorrow I will see Sad. I will get a gun. I will load it. I will get a car, and I will get a credit card. I will do what I gotta do. The door opened, and we walked down the hall to the room. Lamont opened the door.

We entered the suite. Lamont dropped down on the living room couch. I walked off into the bedroom. Shut the door. I looked around at the alien environment. I stood still in the middle of the room. I already missed the walking motion of the machine. My head bobbed a little. I could have walked all night. All night. Why not. I can't dance. I stood in the middle of the room staring at nothing. Nothing. In the wall mirror I still looked pale and white and statue-like. To the left there was a big window overlooking Jersey. I saw myself in the glass like a ghost. Half there. Half not. That is me. And like a mannequin. Odd. Usually other people are the mannequins, not me.

I stood there. I need a gun. I need it loaded. I have business to tend to.

******

In the morning, Lamont Cranston-Fox and I walked off the elevator and into the lobby, bound for the restaurant where Peter and Sad were meeting us for breakfast. It was a typical business morning in an expensive hotel full of all kinds of overdressed people stressing out over their morning meetings. Lamont sat by Peter and started talking with him.

"Gomer says hey," I said to Sad, sitting at their table.

She stared at me. Cold. Of course. How would a South African know that Gomer Pyle frequently said, "hey?"

"How are you?"

"Ok," I said. "Your filings?"

"I have filed them Rusty, and they are on the fast track because the execution is pending. I am not confident. They are all the typical briefs we always file, and they are always quashed. I may be able to squeeze a week or two more for him out of it just because it takes that long to get final decisions recorded at the court clerk's office."

"I have a faster track."

"I've heard about your visit to the car salesman."

"I need to visit the two lying witnesses."

"I know. Peter will…"

"No. I need to visit them as only I can visit them. Alone. You cannot expose Peter or Lamont to my kind of visit. And, above all, you…you cannot be associated with my kind of visitation."

She stared at me. "I will not let you go alone."

"You have to let me go alone. If you want to save this guy I have to go to work alone, and it has to be fast. You followed here today?" I turned to Peter and raised my voice. "You followed here today?"

"No."

"Hmm. Because they will follow you. They will pick you up at your office or your house, and they will follow you. They will kill me the first instant they can get me now. They know I am with you."

I turned back to Sad, "I need a gun. I need bullets. A car and a credit card or cash."

She set her coffee down and sat back in her chair as only her tall, slinky self could do. There are a lot of bells and whistles in a lady's head like Sad's. They were all ringing and blowing.

"Breakfast? Ready to order?" A waitress appeared and asked.

"Two eggs over easy, bacon, toast, whatever you call that breakfast …and a waffle. Do you have waffles?" I asked.

"Yes we do."

"Well then a waffle, too. And coffee."

"I'll have the same," Sad said.

The waitress turned to Peter and Lamont.

"I will do this, on one condition," Sad said. "You have another shock treatment and more pills."

My turn to stare.

"You will need a number of shock treatments and these pills." She opened a leather carry case resting beside her chair leg, reached in and pulled out another Zulu pill. She handed it to me.

I popped it in my mouth and took her glass of water for a short swig.

"It's a deal. The shock doc did me some good. It gave me my appetite back, that's all. Makes me appreciate things like waffles. A few more visits, and I might start watching the Knicks again. May get my sex life back, too." Oh, she wanted to smile at that one. I could tell. But she wouldn't.

"We will visit Dr. Suliman from here. I'll get what you need. You can leave tomorrow."

"The Apes will be watching for me at Suliman's."

"We are meeting him at another office."

"They are following him, too." I warned.

"Have you been sleeping, Rusty? You get any rest last night?"

"I think I feel asleep standing up, thanks for asking."

"Standing up?"

"I woke up and I was standing in the middle of the room. I think I drank a tonic for a cat."

"A tonic for…"

"Yeah, a catatonic. It made me sleep standing up."

She did smile, but she shook it off.

"I have plans for you Rusty, after this. Important plans."

"Do they involve your hero Nelson Mandela?"

"No, they do not. But they are very Mandela-like."

"Peter said he liked Mandela." I leaned forward toward her. "I am not sure I like Peter. He is a mystery to me. Too calm."

"He is very calm. He has been in many wars. Many commando raids in Africa. Not much excites Peter. You will see Peter in a different light as time passes. The tougher things get, the more Peter comes through. He told me you were worried about his reputation at the car salesman's house. He is an extremely loyal friend and ally."

"Well then, I like him more already."

"Rusty, you cannot screw this up. You need to be sane and cautious."

The waitress brought my coffee. Okay. A little sugar and cream. Hilton coffee. Ummm. Good.

"You need to be responsible to the mission of saving this man by gathering information," she said. "My mission is to have the governor order a stay of execution. We can sort out the details later, present a case, when we have more time."

"Yes, meaning the ends justify the ways."

Peter laughed at something Lamont said.

"The Hulk laughs and smiles," I spoke up. And he looked at me.

"I've known you for four days now and that is the first time you haven't looked like a heavy in a black and white war movie."

He stayed smiling and shook his head.

The waitress brought the food over. A waffle smothered in butter was placed before my wicked intentions.

"Whipped cream. I need some whipped cream," I told her. Now I was smiling. Sad even smiled and shook her head, too. Did I sound like a schoolgirl or what? Just get the cream!

Now, where were we going next again?

CHAPTER 14
I GOT A GUN AND IT IS LOADED

In a black BMW, we drove down to the Jersey Shore. All the way down, the Zulu pill painted a jalapeño layer across my brain. Felt like someone spray painted the inside of my skull with Mexican red peppermint. Ocheewawa!

"I saw something on the news last night. The World Sperm Bank is no longer accepting donations from red-headed people," I reported. This had been troubling me.

Sad turned to me and raised an eyebrow.

"In Ireland ten percent of the sperm requested is still red-headed," she said.

"This is true," Peter said. "I saw this feature."

"What does it mean for the clan? What does this mean for mankind? Designer humans."

"That's just the World Sperm Bank, Rusty. I am certain that plenty of red heads will be multiplying outside of the sperm trade."

"I remember that old TV commercial 'the redhead is dead'," I said, as I noticed the sign for Oceanside Heights.

I took my kids and wife there once, but not this far south of the main tourist area, way past the amusement pier. As we drove deeper into the city from the highway, the streets looked like a science fiction movie. Like it was bombed from aliens from Mars.

"Where were you when Sandy hit?" Sad asked.

"Sandy. Sandy. Sandy, the hurricane Sandy? Oh, I was in Camdem and Philly." I really was preoccupied though by looking at the smashed houses and stores. Some were perfect, then right next to them sat piles of rubble.

"I won't ask what you were doing in Camdem," Sad said.

"It rained in Camdem, and Philly."

"Just rained? You are lucky."

Way down on the south side of this city and toward the coast was peppered with ruins. Peter turned us onto a narrow street with new and old condos under construction and some other buildings. It was hard to tell what was being replaced, what was destroyed and what was new. We pulled into a driveway of one, two-story building with a sign that read Welch Clinic and Hospice.

I stepped out of the car. The street had grit and small and big pieces of trash on it. The boardwalk and the beach were at the end of the street. What was once a boardwalk anyway. It was a mass of twisted rubble. Though windy, with a chill in the air, it was still a beautiful day. There were seagulls flying above and that unique sound of nearby waves crashing on the shoreline. You could smell the water in the air. Right up my nose. My nostrils were wide open.

"Am I dying, and no one's told me?" I rapped two knuckles on the hospice sign. No response. Perhaps they were tired of my repartee?

We walked up the steps and into the clinic which showed little sign of being damaged, and into the empty waiting room. We walked right past a smiling receptionist who waved us on like a hand model in a game show. Sad led the way, followed by me, then Peter. We turned into an office, and there I saw a strange man in a medical smock.

"Hello," he said to all of us.

He looked at me.

"And I am told that you cannot recognize me, Rusty. I am the same Dr. Suliman. The same doctor you've met before and that treated you."

He wasn't. He was a different person. Was this a game Sad was playing with me? A test? He held out his hand, and I did not want to shake it. This guy was a total stranger just like the last total strangers I met that called themselves Suliman. I felt a little dizzy right then. A little sick to my stomach.

"We had to change locations for security reasons, Rusty. I assure you that you will be fine here." He touched an intercom on the wall and asked for a nurse."

In walked Nurse Ratshit, I mean Marchant, and I felt better about the set-up.

"It's Miss Muscle Relaxer 1995!" I said. I didn't want to call her Ratshit anymore. Maybe she hadn't seen the Nicholson movie and didn't understand my colorful reference? And…you know. Never mess with someone who gets to stick needles in spinal cords for a living.

"1995? I am not that old Rusty."

"I know." I feigned resignment. There, I insulted her anyway.

"Follow me."

"Where're we going?"

We walked down the hallway, and I brain-prepped myself for another two days of hideously sore muscles. The whole place smelled intensely of peppermint and cleaning fluid.

"Right in here and put on the charming pajamas there on the bed. I'll be right back."

She left. I slipped my expensive loafers off. Did I really

want to do this again? I did…

"You can't!"

I heard the yell down the hall. Then a demanding shriek. "STOP!"

From the receptionist? I listened and heard a crash. I pulled my pants back up.

"Hey, you can't…" This time it was Dr. Frankenstein's voice.

I peeked outside and down the hall. The yelling was now in the office I'd just left. The hand model receptionist was standing by the front door. Cowering. Hair messed up. Crying. She'd been roughed up!

In socks, I walked down the hall.

"BAM!"

Oh, now that was a damn gun. A gunshot! A man groaned. Who? Peter? The Doc? More yelling.

I heard a yelp. The nurse, Marchant was behind me, and I turned to see her standing half in a doorway, frightened. I ran back to her.

"Scissors," I whispered one word. She stepped into the room and came back with a big silver pair. I winked. I ran down near the first office doorway. People were still arguing inside. A man groaned, an animal groan. And of course, the yelling was all about me.

"Where is he?" a man demanded. Familiar voice.

"Where!" another yelled.

The receptionist still stood down the hall by the front clutching the neck of her clothing. I put a finger to my lips making that intergalactic hand signal of – "keep your freakin' mouth shut."

I was at the office door, making my plan. I thought about disconnecting the scissors into two knives and then…

…a man barged right out of the room, head forward. Right into me, in the hall. He wore a fedora hat and raincoat. Angry face. Angry pace. It was Detective Macelroy! He was looking for me and sure-the-fuck-surprise! There I was! He found me inches away. With silver scissors inches from his naked throat. He had his pistol in his hand. I grabbed it. He was still way surprised. And I shoved the scissors straight into the front of his throat. Deep. How deep? The tip must have hit the spinal cord, that's how deep. I could feel the crunch. I'd had enough of him. He let go of his gun, and I still held it in my left hand, as he clutched his throat with both of his hands. He could barely even gag. I guess it's hard to gag when you have a big ass pair of scissors flat through your windpipe and throat.

I uprighted the pistol in my hand and turned the corner into the room. Detective Cranston was there alright. He held his gun aimed at Sad. Peter stood a few feet away. Doc was down in the corner on the floor, moaning. I absolutely knew that when Cranston saw me, he would turn the gun on me as an instinct.

"Evening dipshit," I growled.

And he did. He took the barrel off Sad and started to turn it toward me. From my hip I unloaded on this scum bastard. I blew him up. Blew up his face. His neck and his chest. He fell back, and I watched his gun hand because you know, he could still shoot. But he dropped the pistol. Then he dropped his life. He fell to the floor.

Sad and Peter just stood there. Sad's mouth hung open. Peter was cool. He stepped to her and held her arm. Then Macelroy fell back into view in the doorway, with a big honking pair of shiny scissors in his Adam's apple.

Sad and Peter turned to Dr. Suliman. I stepped out into the hallway and motioned for the nurse and the receptionist to come in to help them.

"Where's the bullet?" I asked.

"Shoulder," Peter said, and he ripped open the shirt on

Doc's chest. Sad knelt down. Without looking up, Peter ordered, "Get the medical room ready."

"We should call the police!" the receptionist said.

"Honey, they are the police. Were the police," I corrected. "But as you can see they walked right in and shot your boss right in the chest. They are, were, the bad police. And they would have killed all of us before they left."

She stared at me. She was lost. Scrambled. My words were fine. Her brains weren't.

"So, we are not calling the police. Get it?" I finished. "The police will come and kill us."

"Nor, an ambulance," the Doc mumbled from the floor in a sigh.

She looked at Sad's face for guidance. Sad's face looked sad. Very sad, her lips formed in a downturn, and she shook her head side-to-side. The hand model lady finally understood that the police just could not be called. And what she saw around her was all the help she was going to get.

I made a quick study of the carcass that was once Cranston. He had about half a face left, and he was door-nail-dead. I picked up his gun. Macelroy was through gagging out in the hall. Two dead, bad cops. Two cops, nonetheless. And this was a lose-lose mess. I moved over to Peter and helped lift the Doc up. We started out of the room and down the hall to wherever I guessed the best medical room in this building was. The nurse suddenly stepped into view ahead of us and beckoned us to her.

I assume between you guys you can fix him up?" I asked. Peter said nothing.

"We can," Sad said. "I am a doctor, but Peter is a combat surgeon. He has lots of experience with gunshot wounds."

He glanced at me and nodded. Sad was right earlier. I really am liking Peter more and more. We laid the doc down on a medical, operating table, or bed of some kind, and the nurse, Sad and Peter went to work on him.

"I'm going to see if they were alone," I said out loud, but really to Peter. He nodded.

"You got this?" I asked.

"I got it," Peter nodded.

I stepped over to him and shoved Cranston's pistol in the small of Peter's back inside the beltline of his pants. Peter and I knew. Cause you know...this shit ain't over yet. Anyone backing them up outside expected to hear gunshots in the building, as we were all to be killed. But within a reasonable amount of time if their guys didn't return, they'd come and check.

I turned to see the receptionist standing crying in the doorway.

"Come here," I said softly as I passed her. "Walk with me."

"What's your name?" I asked. I ducked into the prep room and slipped on my shoes.

"Evelyn."

"Evelyn, we are going to pretend you were not here tonight. If you whisper this to anyone...well...you will be killed by some of these guys...these guys..."

We walked to Macelroy's body. I did a quick pat down. Two magazines on his belt and one in his coat pocket. Nice raincoat.

"...these guys are like the Mafia. You know the Mafia?" She nodded.

"These guys are like the Mafia. They work with the Mafia. And if they thought you were here? They would kill you. You would just...disappear. Like the people you hear about on the news. Disappear. Okay?"

We walked to the front waiting room.

"You cannot tell anyone. No one about this. No one. And right now, I want you to go back by Peter in the operating room back there. Okay? You will be safe by Peter. Okay?"

"Okay."

"Okay."

She left me. Poor kid. Must be hell having a soul and a conscience. I peered out some of the waiting room windows. Looked the street over for the cars. There were cars lined up on both sides of the street. Most looked trashed out from the storm and some didn't. They didn't follow us here. They must have followed Suliman here. Now he's shot for it. Shot for helping me, whichever version he is today. I told them he would be followed. I warned them. It was getting dusk out there.

I returned to Macelroy's body and rolled his torso out of his raincoat. Then I picked up his fedora. Hey, why not? We were about the same size. Wrong color hair though. I put the hat and coat on. Pressed the hat down flatter and lifted the collar. If it got a little darker out, could I walk on the street and see if these chumps had backup in a car? Would they think I was Macelroy? Could I get close?

I looked out a side window and down the street. It was getting darker. There were a few vacation condo houses still standing on the block, intact, but they all looked dark. Then I looked over the empty businesses. Some were damaged and closed. A small apartment complex fenced off and under reconstruction. Closed real estate office…and… wait! General Grant! General Ulysses S. Grant was out there on the street. Standing on the street? Where has he been? He stood there, smoking a cigar right by a sedan. A four-door sedan. Yeah. It was the NYPD detective sedan brand. It even had the extra antenna. Yeah. I kind of broadened my vision out, looking at not one thing and seeing everything. This is the best way to pick up unusual motion in normal stillness. Patterns and things breaking patterns.

Something moved in the sedan, and my eyes picked it up. Our third man. The driver. I jogged down the hall and went out the back door. The clinic had a yard, full of storage stuff. To the right was the apartment complex under construction. If I could maybe…I jumped up on a wall and clung to a chain link fence until I inched down to a corner where several fence corners converged…could I maybe get west of this car, behind it on the street? I squeezed through the corners of the fence and dropped onto the back parking lot of the complex. I ran to its west end. I got up on the west wall and looked over it. A business backyard. Looked deserted to me. It had washed up rubble and trash in it.

Jump. Jump again. I'm in. I ran the yard and turned by the building and ran up the alley. There was another gate but, with a pull on the gate handle, I was right out on the street. I was now west and behind my new buddy in the getaway car. I hit the sidewalk and walked further west, briskly. Down at the avenue, I crossed over to his side of the street and walked down his sidewalk side, trying to stay out of his rear-view mirror.

I pulled down the hat, pulled up the collar and jogged, got closer, then ran up to the car and, as I passed it, I pounded a flat hand hard on the hood of the car and growled, "Come on!"

And I ran like hell for the boardwalk. I sure hoped it was dark enough. I hoped that I'd looked enough like Macelroy in the dark to lure him out. I heard a car door and some running feet behind me. He was coming. Come on, come on, come on. I was getting close to the wrecked boardwalk. Despite the hurricane damage, I could hear and see the amusement park north of us was open way up the boardwalk.

I got under the mangled, broken boardwalk and turned a sharp left, and it was as ratty and rough there as I expected it to be. Junk. Beams and supports. Metal racks. Dark. Busted up wood. I got right behind a support beam. Pulled the gun from my pocket. North and a bit above me I could hear the rollercoaster at the amusement park rocking around the curves. Kids screaming at a distance. Our third ape turned the same corner I had, in a half dark silhouette, and I shot him fast.

He crashed down on his arms headfirst, like he was diving into second base. But he was diving into sand, rocks and pieces of wood, not baseball diamond dirt. I started to step out when the son of a bitch shot right back at me! Yeah! He was that good. Yeah! He'd rolled and drew his sidearm like a movie star and shot back at me!

I jumped back behind the beam. The bullets tore through the air by me. He was slow to get up. He was bent over at that point, and all I saw of him was his left hip and ass. I shot. I hit the hip good. He groaned real good and slithered forward and out of my sight. But I had to follow him. What if he called for help on a phone or radio? And, I had to pursue in his exact trail to see him best.

Gun forward, I leaped and dodged the debris trying to chase him up ahead. I could hear him snaking away. A leg! I saw a leg and, before it disappeared, I shot it. I caught it. He groaned out again. He shot again. I ducked, but the round hit the boardwalk floor above us. He was trying to slow me down.

I stepped to the side a bit and then rushed forward. He was just a few feet ahead in an awkward position, all wounded and worried about me behind him, yet trying to escape. I shot instantly. The bullet went through the top of his shoulder and into his head. He gasped. He tried to turn his gun on me, but he dropped it and flopped around.

I couldn't shoot again. Couldn't risk the noise. I sat down and watched him gurgle off and die. It happened fast. He was a young guy. Late twenties. Short hair. And here was his end. In the muck. On some rocks, sand and scattered trash and rubble all under a broken boardwalk.

How does a guy join NYPD and in 6 or 8 years or so come to this end? Here. Tonight? Driving two other cops to the Jersey shore to commit murder, to cover up other murders and drug smuggling? I picked up his pistol and patted him down. I didn't take his wallet. I didn't want to see, you know, the family photos and shit inside – the people he'd been lying to for years about who he really was...what he was really doing.

I looked north, saw the whole run of the twisted underbelly of the boardwalk until it became a pitch-black pit on the horizon point. And you know, I thought about just walking off. Just walking off from all of this. Stealing a car. Going back to Jersey City and selling some crack. Maybe Baltimore. But I cussed aloud. I couldn't. Sad needed me. And Steverino needed me. I stood up over this guy. What a mess I was in, and what a mess the world was in, too. His cell phone started to ring. I snatched it up. It was a Manhattan phone number. I took the phone and buried it into my armpit to stifle the ring. Bums often live under these boardwalks. But hey, hadn't I made enough noise already?

Three dead bodies. A shot doctor. An abandoned police car. A receptionist freaking out. Peter and I had a lot of cover-up to do tonight. A lot.

Okay, what was I supposed to do next?

CHAPTER 15
SAILOR TAKE WARNING

Dawn.

Dawn on the rocky beach. I sat on a big grey rock, amongst hundreds of big grey rocks. The morning tide lopped in the crevices all around me. It was a red sky. Red sky at morning, sailor take warning. Red sky at night. Sailor's delight. Hey, my dad was in the Navy. I know these things.

It was wet and chilly, but with the collar up on my dead copper's raincoat, I was just fine. I was exhausted. And, I was at some peace. Odd. Finally. Sitting here of all places. I bet I would not sleep standing up tonight. Long night. A very long night. We drowned the three bodies. Guns too, which was a real shame. I hate wasting good guns. Cleanliness matters when you shoot people.

Did I say three guns? Don't tell anyone I kept Macelroy's pistol. I kept the pistol I snatched from his hand. Yeah, ballistic-wise, if they find the bodies, and I get caught with this gun, a cop's gun, I am in deep-dish trouble. I know. I know. This pistol in my pocket, its serial number is probably recorded in the NYPD books as Macelroy's. But I have a plan for this gun. In facta-mundo, I plan on having it engraved with Macelroy's name in fact. So, I convinced Peter to let me keep it. I would have to part with my nice, raincoat soon though. Maybe when the sun was really up, and I was toasty warm.

We drove out to the Melway Rock Quarry. It's a special place I know of in south Jersey where mobsters ditch cars and dead punks that screw up. We ditch 'em, in their car into about 300 feet of fresh water. In about 30 years they will build a shopping center there, drain the quarry and find the missing car and all kinds of bad guys, all with the consistency of clam chowder. Maybe even Jimmy Hoffa soup?

We got back to the clinic at about 6 a.m. and, rather than go in with Peter, I took a stroll under the boardwalk and out to the shoreline of big rocks. Drawn to the water like a maggot, ah, I mean a magnet. I just wanted to sit by myself for a while, but I soon heard Peter walking up, and that's okay. This Peter guy was growing on me.

I turned to him and winced and grunted as he navigated the rock tops and handed me a cup of carry-out coffee from the WaWa store. He sat down a few feet away with his own cup, on his own little rock island.

"Tired, me bucko?" I said.

"Tired," Peter said.

"Last week I was knocking down old ladies for their change purse. Now I'm killing cops for Jesus."

My twisted biography just seems to continue. I peeled back the lid and sipped the coffee. It was black. That was good.

"You look like hell," I said.

"Feel like it, too."

"How's the Doc?"

"Resting. Resting. He is patched up really well. He needs to make some new blood."

I nodded. "Don't we all?"

The small waves worked around our feet and rocks.

"How's Sad?"

"She's fine." He sipped his coffee. "Sad is very tough. She has seen a lot in her life. She was tortured as a teenager by the government. She was gang-raped by soldiers. Sad is a very tough woman."

You know I got kind of tongue-tied over that part. Gang-raped by soldiers?

"She supported the doctor all night. He doesn't even have a fever," Peter added.

"Bullet out?"

"The bullet is out."

"You learn all that in the South African Army?"

"The emergency medicine? Yes, I did."

"You see a lot of action there?"

"Yes, I did. Up north. In the Congo. We were sent all over. But there was a lot of action inside our country, too. A lot of bad action. Para Bat. Special Forces."

"Para ....Bat?"

"Paratrooper Battalion."

"Bad action," I repeated. "How did you meet Sad?"

He was quiet for a moment. He looked at me and eyed me over real good, like maybe he was thinking about telling me the truth, or if I was worthy of hearing the long answer and not the short one. That kind of eyeing-over. Seen it many times while taking confessions. And disposing of bodies creates a certain...camaraderie. A certain bonding. Maybe I deserve the long answer?

"In the military," he said, now eyeing the horizon.

"She was in the military, too?"

"No." He sipped more coffee.

The sun got a bit higher. Seagulls got a bit louder. I watched some fly over us. I guess I was not getting the truth or the long answer.

"I was one of the soldiers that raped her," he said quietly.

DAMN! I was even more tongue-tied over that! What?

"Raped...her? Sad?"

"Yes, Rusty..."

"How are you two..."

"Working together? Friends?"

"Yeah."

"I wasn't much older than she was at the time. Young fool. I was with my mates, and they weren't much older. We were sent into an area, a mining city where the proper votes for a leader were not cast. There was a run-off. We were to ...visit...the small city and make a statement."

"The statement included that? Rape?"

"The statement of the administration included many things. People were killed. People disappeared. Family members...killed. Arrested. Tortured. Raped."

It got real quiet out there on the coast. I was not pushing the confession. Confessions are like the tide. Like music. You can't rush them. The move in when they move in.

"A few years passed," he continued. "I became a Sergeant. I few things happened to me. In my life. I guess you could say, I saw the error of my ways? My evils. My mistakes. Many things of my doing."

"Find Jesus?"

"No."

"That...kind of thing."

"Yes. Something happened to me. I guess you could say, I changed. I saw a movie. A stupid, corny movie. But I saw it at the right time, I guess. I realized I could not undo all the things I'd done. But, I tried to undo some. I remembered Sad for some reason, how we caught her, when we caught her. I...," he got quiet. The Afrikaner was choked up. So was I.

"After some years I sought her out. I found her. I found her and her mother in Pretoria. Like a fool I came with flowers. Like some fool. I begged her forgiveness. Begged. Her mother wanted to shoot me in their kitchen. But Sad…"

"She forgave you?"

"She…forgave me. And I swore I would… I would be at her side to help her. To support her. I helped pay for her college and for her medical school. Sad must have seen something in me that was worth forgiving. I wound up helping her in her many causes in South Africa. Missing people. Medicines to the poor. Crimes. All in my official capacities in the Army and police. Officially and unofficially, too. Many times in secret."

"Like this Underground Railroad of helpers you guys have now."

"Yes."

"And then Mandela came along."

"Yes. Mandela came along. Sad has been like a freedom fighter. She is quite brilliant. She is like this rock." He rapped his knuckles on the little rock island upon which he sat. "It is an ugly business. True justice. True freedom."

"And true forgiveness," I mumbled.

"And true forgiveness."

"Well, you are a soldier for the cause now, Peter."

"And so are you, Rusty."

That gave me a real chill, even under the dead cop's jacket.

"Oooooh no, no, no, no, I am crazy, Peter. I can't be trusted, and I can't even trust myself," I blurted out. "I cannot be forgiven for the things I have done. By nobody. By Jesus. By nobody."

"You have been injured. You, you've lost your real self. But now, something is happening in your mind, Rusty. Something is trying to heal itself. Something is working itself out. It is not unlike my change. That is why you walked into our foundation. Why you found us."

"I don't know. You don't know what it's like being in here with me. Being me. I am all like…like radio static with rusty, razor blades."

Peter stood up. He looked at the waves. I stood up on my rock, too.

"I trust you," he said.

I looked at him.

"I trust you as far as I can throw you," he added with a half-smile.

"Well, considering you're the freaking Hulk, that's pretty far."

"Let's get to the clinic. Collect the Doc and Sad. We have to move out. Maybe to a place in Pennsylvania today."

"What movie was that, the one you saw that changed you?"

"An American Western. 'Shane'."

"Shane." I made a mental note to watch that again sometime. A movie for defining moments, I guess.

"It is the troubadour, the actor, the writer that explains our lives back to us," I mumbled.

He stopped and looked at me.

"Ah, it's just something I use to say."

He smiled. We walked across the rocks, under the boardwalk, across some sand and onto this cursed street I hope never to see again. On the sidewalk, my eyes, my vision suddenly…like clicked over from HD to small screen, like that, best way I can describe it. Like a switch in my eyes. Not accurate, but the best way. I think my Zulu pill was wearing of. I rubbed my eyes. I was having another internal problem again. Damn!

"The Five Apes and the Mob think we're dead right now. But when they don't hear from their goombas, they'll get suspicious by lunchtime. That was my best guess," I managed to say from inside my tunnel vision relapse.

Peter agreed.

We walked up the sidewalk. I glanced over my shoulder. General Grant was now up on the crushed boardwalk. Near where we sat. I wonder if he heard everything we said?

Inside, we walked straight to the operating room. We found Nurse Ratshit asleep in a chair. Sad was up by the good doctor who was laid out in bed. Evidence of a gunshot wound told me he was the same doctor because damned if he wasn't a different dude to me again! Looked different. Confused, I shook my head. But it had to be him. It was like having to believe an LSD trip was real.

Sad looked at me, and I looked at her. I reflexively winked at her and gave her a small smile. There was always a lot of life in her face. Her face was never flat you know? But this time, even though, like my eyes weren't on cue? Her face was deeper to me. Deeper. Deep.

I just hugged her, you know? She had been through a lot. Since she was a kid even, and a lot just last night, too. I'd been through a lot, too, but I am just a piece of shit.

"We gotta go," I whispered.

"Right after your shock treatment," Sad said.

"Seriously?"

"Seriously."

"Well, crank up the juice box, Ratshit." I declared. "I got a lightning date with destiny!"

CHAPTER 16
TOODLES

I sat up at 8:30 a.m. and turned on the bed and put my bare feet down on the bear skin rug. It was morning in Pennsylvania. Every muscle in my body ached again from the shock treatment. My toenails hurt. How long can I do this? Who needs a gym workout? A shock treatment every three days, and in six months I'll be Captain America.

Through the window, I saw trees moving in the wind. Some drizzling rain. Some buildings of a small, city skyline off in the distance. I was in another strange, new place. I was alone. Alone. It hit me. Alone again, naturally. For some ungodly reason, I had a flash back of a rainy day in New York City in the 1980s. Me driving my first car. It was more of a feeling than a flashback. I was alone in the car. A Sunday morning. A teenager. I just had to get in my car and get outside Manhattan and drive up to Bear Mountain. I was alone then and had an idea on that drive I would end up alone someday. In the end. We all do, don't we? Somebody famous said we all die alone. Maybe like that kid under the boardwalk. I remember the feeling on that drive. The isolation. And now, I felt like I would be alone the whole rest of my life. Driving in the rain that day. An omen come true. My mother had died when I was very young. And now, I remembered that my father died, too, but recently, Rich said. He's gone. Now my wife, well my ex-wife, hides from me, hides behind an actress. My kids are ghosts to me. They are like adults now with no memory of me. I am the ghost.

I bolted from the bed and jumped to the window, like the bed was a hot stove on my bare ass. I stood naked at the window, gasping, with my hands on the window frame. I was suffocating. The rain did not help. We die alone. And if I came back as a single drop of rain, the song says I will remain. But I don't think so. A drop of rain? I'll scream all the way down. If I hit the water? I'll drown. If I hit the ground? I'll smash into a million pieces.

A knock on the door. My God, it's 9:45!

The door opened, "Rusty?"

It was Sad.

I was naked, but I didn't care. She didn't care either. She walked in and sat in a chair. She held a glass of water in her hand. I sat back on the bed.

"How are you this morning?"

"Depressed," I quickly answered. "Depressed. Ahhh. Alone? Alone."

She nodded.

"I am just crushed. I am alone," I blurted out.

"Not even the General?"

"Ah," I groaned. "Not even the General will sit with me."

"Do you feel empty and hollow?"

"Jeez, that was fast. That some kind of post, electric shock test question?"

She half-smirked and canted her head. "Hmmm, yes, it is. Sorry."

"This is my own personal insanity, Sad. Everyone owns their own insanity. It shouldn't be easily deciphered in a few test questions."

"Yes," she said.

"Pass? Fail?" I still had to ask.

"Are you hearing voices?"

"Yours." That was too smart-ass. "I don't."

"When you see General Grant, does he ever speak?"

"No."

"Do you hear anything? His feet shuffle? A draw on his cigar? Any sound?"

"No. He just sits there. But one time, one time I saw two dead men on a park bench, not that long ago, and one of them was singing."

"The brain often compensates for deficiencies. You have heard of the Phantom Limb? If there is a problem with visual or auditory functioning, hallucinations may compensate. It is the brain working through its problems."

I shook my complicated head.

"Sorry, Rusty. Your mind has been set on fire. Your mind is also healing. Parts of it are. You are going to be flooded with a great many emotions. They will take you by surprise. You have to be prepared for floods of ideas and emotions. Memories. Prepare yourself for this. For some people, the prognosis is a new calm. A calming. For others, the opposite."

"The prior life of an unemotional psychopath was so clear and simple," I bemoaned.

"Hmmmm," she reached over and handed me a big pill and the glass of water. I took it. I took the Zulu pill and chased it with the whole glass of water.

"How's the Doc this morning?" I asked, staring ahead at the wall. I then realized I was still sitting there balls-ass naked. I pulled a blanket over me.

"He is much better. He is up and about a bit. We gave him his appropriate shots last night."

"Lead poisoning shot?" Oh, that was funny. To me, anyway.

"His life is screwed now. They will come after him when they learn all three of their guys are missing. They will kidnap him or something. They'll get the Mob to do it, or an especially sicko cop to do it. I have seen their work." I tipped the glass up to get the last drops of water. "It ain't like in the movies, well maybe a Tarentino movie."

The pill hit the ol' gut hard. I burped, and it tasted bad. Like purple licorice. "If they find out he's been shot? They'll know he was at the center of a nasty disappearance. And your life! Your life is screwed, too."

Sad just sat there, calmly. Her prognosis was calm.

"Peter and I are going into work at the Manhattan office this afternoon. Business as usual, but with some extra security around. Work as usual. They will not confront me. We will leave some security here with you. The good doctor, too."

I shook my head, because that was such a temporary solution. "These guys wait ten years to kill you."

"We are going to pick up what you need and get back here with it. Maybe tomorrow, you'll feel up to making that visit to New England."

"They will follow you."

"We will lose them."

"Then they will follow your security people. I'm telling you."

"Rusty, you need to relax. Peter is handling all of that."

"Do I have any clothes? Where are my clothes?"

"Peter burned everything. He is buying you some clothes this morning."

"Okay," I nodded. They needed burning. And the ashes spread coast to coast. "I need a pistol."

"You already have a pistol. Peter found it."

"I need that pistol."

"For what?"

"An end game. No, not my end. I am not suicidal. I will kill everyone else first and then me last. I want to stuff it somewhere for a while. Hide it. An ace in the hole for an end game. I need another pistol. I need a hat. A fedora like the detective wore. I can't be seen in the city with my Conan O'Brien red hairdo streaming wild. Sunglasses. Dress gloves. I need a small tape recorder and small video cam."

"You've thought this out."

"No, I haven't. Not really."

"Are you hungry?"

"I have thought that out. Bacon and eggs. Pancakes or a waffle. Coffee with cream AND sugar."

"Wrap yourself up in that blanket," she said while standing. "Come on downstairs, and let's see what kind of insane cook you are."

I grimaced. "Me?"

"Did you think I can cook, too?" she asked in response to my expression.

"No? Your multi-tasking doesn't include making me breakfast?"

Okay! Every strand of muscle in me felt sore. I am telling you that you can start a new TV infomercial about losing weight and gaining muscle. The new Shock Treatment 9000 from the savannahs of Africa. Or how about...Shocka Zula?

We walked downstairs, me in the rear like a Roman in a toga. Friends, Romans, countrymen, lend me your underwear. Boxers, or briefs.

"Dr Suliman, I presume?" I asked of the strange man with a chest bandage stretched out on the living room couch watching TV. He smiled. Damned if he didn't look different yet again. Crack security agent Lamont Cranston-Foxx was there next to him in a lounge chair.

"Shouldn't you be across the street in a tree scanning the neighborhood with binoculars?" I asked him.

"How do you know my partner isn't there right now?" The smart-ass answered. I should have chopped his throat in two the other night in the elevator ... Chop-chop.

"Where were you last night when we needed you?" I continued as I limped past him.

"How are you this morning, Rusty?" the man disguised as Suliman asked.

"Peachy keen. Yourself?"

"It hurts to breathe."

"Join the club."

I followed Sad into the kitchen. It was a nice house. An elderly, white woman with short-cropped gray hair, sat at the kitchen table working on a laptop.

"This is Agnes," Sad said.

I nodded.

"She owns the house."

I nodded.

"Whatever is mine, is Sad's," the lady said. "Then it is yours."

Sad shook her head at the hospitality. I guessed Agnes was another in Sad's Underground Railroad. Somebody she helped at some point.

"Young man, you look like you need some coffee."

"Like…like…real bad as a matter of fact."

"Sit down, son." She hauled her heavyset self out of the chair and waddled to the kitchen. She poured me a cup of coffee.

I sat at the table, on a wooden chair with a plaid, plastic-covered, cushion that whooshed when I buried my ass into it. She carried the coffee to me, and I added the cream and sugar from little ceramic containers shaped like cartoon lambs.

"I know you are hungry."

"I am."

"Miss Sad, are you hungry?"

"I am, Agnes."

"Well, sit yourself down too, honey."

Sad reached toward a counter and pulled out a stack of newspapers, sat and tossed them in front of us. Before I realized it, I instinctively reached toward the stack and slid some sections over to me. The smell of bacon circulated. TV in the background. Coffee was great. It was something like Christmas. If I only had some boxers on. And slippers. Oh, I mean moccasins.

I wondered if I could live here?

I wondered if I could freeze this beautiful moment?

I wondered if I could live on Zulu pills?

I wondered what I was going to do tomorrow with a car and a gun, and a fedora. A New England trip? Did I forget some part of the plan?

******

The next morning, we stood in the detached garage behind Agnes's house. I was being briefed by a guy named Decorvio from Sad's New York office about all the new cool gear I was getting. Like he was Q in a Bond flick. Sad was there paying attention to how much I was paying attention but, as you can see, I was also paying attention to her paying attention, too. Paying attention is a full-time job!

Nothing too techno going on, just discussions on papers, where my new socks were and where the money was. I had on my new Dillards' duds, a black leather zipper jacket over a brown shirt. Black pants, nice shoes and thick socks. I think I may hire Peter to buy all my clothes. A suitcase on the ground was probably full of more of the same. A dark fedora, as requested, was on the dashboard of my new set of wheels, a Mercedes Benz. What? Naaah, just kidding, it was a tan Camry. Whew. Super-spy! But this a great, non-descript car for worming around. The new 9mm pistol was shoved into the beltline of my pants, in the small of the back, or S.O.B. as we called it in the business.

Macelroy's police pistol was safely buried in the corner of Agnes's back yard in a zip lock bag. I've got plans for that, you know. I am not just a pretty face under shocking red hair that stands up like a porcupine.

"The files on your passenger side seat are everything we have on Marion Delafasio and Julian Managos," Decorvio said.

I nodded, looking in the window at the...dossiers, Mr. Bond.

"There is a suitcase in the trunk with some cameras."

I nodded.

"Your medicine, "Sad added, "is in a shaving kit in your luggage. One a day."

I nodded.

Decorvio gave me the keys.

"Do you feel like you are sending your kid off to his first day of school?" I asked Sad.

"Worse. But I never had kids, Rusty," Sad said, "I guess this is what it might feel like. Are you alone today?"

"You mean the General? He must be off fighting anoth-er war somewhere."

Sad nodded. Decorvio looked at us both, confused.

I got inside the car. Peter walked across the yard and approached us. He put his hand on Sad's shoulder and leaned a bit toward my window.

"Good luck, my friend," Peter said.

"Bye, Mom and Dad." You guessed it. I almost said, "Toodles."

I drove out of the garage. I saw weird, little-old Agnes on the back porch, looking like a stuffed tomato in polyes-ter. She raised a hand to wave, and I gave her a thumbs up.

Off to investigate. Investigate. Yeah! Okay...now... what was I doing again?

CHAPTER 17
MELTING ON IMPACT

An early fall snow fell on the hilly, downtown Brattleboro, Vermont streets this Sunday evening. I'd followed Julian Managos from his house to this downtown area of closed businesses and some open bars and restaurants. Julian met some friends at the Best Winds Sports Bar. I wandered down to the front door. It was too small a joint for me to walk in and not be seen and noted. All the TVs had the New England Pats game on, and Julian and his buds were all lined up on stools watching the biggest screen. They looked like gumbas to me. But, statistically? That's one to many goombas for Brattleboro.

I couldn't go in. Wanted to but couldn't. I'd shoved my red hair all up into the fedora and had the brim pulled down and my jacket collar turned way up. Can't hang inside there for hours, cooking in clothes like that. And I can't make memories yet either. Too soon.

Probably, homeboy was in there for the whole game. I walked back to my car up the street and drove to a convenience store I'd passed on the way in. Hit the john. Bought some coffee and a ham and cheese sandwich. Drove back to the bar's street, parked near Julian's car and put the game on the radio. Man, that sandwich was good. Packed, store sandwiches really have come a long way, you know? Made fresh daily. The bread was whole grain, thick and spongy. I hit the windshield wiper every few minutes to fling off the snow. The Pats were winning big.

A teenager walked by in a red flannel jacket and one of those Russian style, flap caps. He was thin, gawky and it was easy to see there was something wrong with him. His head jerked side-to-side, and he talked to himself. He would stop and try to collect snow on his hands and then lick them. I hoped he wouldn't see me in the car and come over to me, or something. He wandered the streets in and out of areas where I could see of him. Where were his parents? Why was he out loose?

The game ended. I turned my radio off. Some guys stumbled out into the street. Then Julian and his gumbas left the bar. As they lingered at the front and, with that, the weird teenager walked by them.

"Hey, hey, it's the village idiot!" One of the men shouted.

The boy ignored him, and one of them shoved the kid on his shoulder. The kid freaked. He roared out some mix of words as he regained his balance. He tried to walk on, but another one danced his fat self into the kid's way.

"Hey, water head! Water head boy! Where ya going? Where ya going?"

"Where do you think you're going?" Another shouted.

"Naaaaarhhh!" The kid screamed.

The guys reached down and scooped up snow. They packed snowballs. They threw them at the kid. Laughing. The kid made sounds like he was crying. He flailed at the air trying to swat at the snowballs. Finally he turned up the sidewalk and headed up the hill toward me. The men roared in laughter. The kid passed me, groaning in tears.

I heard them say some goodbyes, and Julian and another guy walked up the sidewalk. They were busy in conversation. Drunk talk. Too loud, and their walk was sloppy. I got out of my car. I pulled my hat down good and my collar up good and wandered down the sidewalk until I got near Julian's car. The two did not notice me until they were about 12 feet away. They stopped.

"Hello, Julian," I said.

He stuck his hands into his coat pockets quickly. I lifted my hands, showed him my palms and spread my fingers.

"You don't need that," I said calmly with a smile.

"Who are you?"

"Tommy. Tommy from New York. The city itself, not the State."

"What you want….up here?"

"They sent me here to check in with you."

"Check in wit me about what?"

I looked over at his friend. He was not a player. He stood there dumfounded with no stance, jaw down like a high school chum or something. I leaned against the front of Julian's Mustang.

"Julian and I need to talk for a minute. Can you give us a minute?" I said to the chum.

"Yeah, yeah Toops, go on, go on. I got this."

"Okay?" he asked.

"Yeah, yeah, okay."

Toops wandered up the street.

I looked at the Mustang, "What happened to the Caddy?"

"The Caddy? That was a long time ago."

And with that remark, he knew that I knew and he felt a little more comfortable. He too sat on the hood of the car. We both looked down the snowy street for a few seconds.

"Julian, do you know that Steverino is going to be executed in about three weeks or so?"

"Yeah, ahhh no. I…didn't know about it in weeks. I knew it was coming, but not three weeks."

"The reason I am here, is that, through the years we have learned that when people are about to be executed in prison…certain people involved in the execution situation… sometimes…get a…oh, whatcha call it…a conscious? They begin to regret. They begin to second guess themselves."

"Dat ain't me, Tommy. You have nothing to worry about, about that at all."

I stared at his face. His eyes. He was right. He could care less. Steverino was like a dog he ran over ten years ago. Maybe even on purpose. You know my standards are low, anymore. And that was a confession to me. It wouldn't work in court. But it worked in my slimy, low world. He did what I thought he did. He just clearly confessed to me.

Julian bounced off the car and smiled.

"You can tell your friends that I am no such problem. That deal is done and forgotten. I forgot about it!" he said.

"I knew it. I knew. But they sent me. You know! They still sent me."

I stood up from the car and walked off toward mine.

See ya around, Julian. Take care of yourself," I said.

"Yeah, yeah, you, too, Tommy. And if I can do anything again, I'm your man."

"You will always be so considered. You work very clean, my friend." Which he did.

He got into his Mustang, cranked the engine and drove off. I got into my car and sat staring down the street. A few more people wandered out of the bar. Said their good-nights. I decided I'd get some coffee and drive a few more hours south through the night. Get out of here. The snow wasn't sticking much on the roads at least. I started up my car and u-turned. I proceeded south. Next stop, New York City, capital of the free universe.

Center of the known universe. But, I couldn't pretend to be in the Mafia down there with Mr. Marion Delafasio, the neighbor of the dead, China Doll. He knew me too well. I took the witness statement from this lying fuck years ago and, no matter how far I pulled this hat down he would know me. Know my face. Even years later. He swore to me that he saw Steverino haul a heavy, rolled carpet out of the neighbor's house and into a red car. Swore an oath. Said it on the stand in the courtroom trial. Earned himself a Caddy and some cash. Then the anonymous Julian up here lied saying he saw the same man, the same car, the same license plate, the carpet and the body buried up here. Sewed up in a Crime Stoppers phone tip. We dug up the body at the Connecticut site. We put two and two together and came up with five and a half. Six even. And I was too blind and stupid to see it.

Steverino came up with a death sentence. And I helped like a punk. Like a fool. Like corrupt scum. A chump in a pretty dark suit and a toy badge. A facsimile for an investigator. A pawn. All like that. They couldn't buy me and Rich, so they fooled us. They laughed at us. At me. They drank beers over me. I fell down for it. Face down. They walked on me. They walked all over me. Then, when they thought I'd wised up? They shot me down like a dog, on purpose and they never looked back.

If Delafasio confesses to me tomorrow, the Five Apes and the Mafia will kill him. If he lies to me, I may kill him. I glanced out the window to my right as I drove off, and I saw that kid again, sitting by some old metal trash cans on the curb. His tongue was sticking out like he was trying to catch snowflakes on it. You'll never catch a snowflake like that, kid. Life melts on impact.

Now…where was I going?

CHAPTER 18
I'M A DEAD MAN

"Murder at a good address." New Yorkers like that. A good sensational murder and a decent, upscale address. It's tabloid heaven. Of course, I haven't stood here in this particular alley in over a decade. The Chinese diplomat Bo Zoup had long ago moved from this house after the murder and who knew who lived there now. New people, probably ignorant of the past horror as New Yorkers are ignorant of the city's haunts on every turn.

I looked at the house next door. Can I catch Delafasio alone? It is hard catching someone alone sometimes. Finding out when they will be alone and having enough time to do your dirty deeds that need doing. I needed such a sublime moment with Mr. Delafasio. It was late evening when I walked down the driveway of the China Doll's old house. The Vermont snow was only a light drizzle of rain down here in the city, and it fell around my feet on the brick driveway that separated the Delafasio house and the Doll house. These were nice houses on a nice street. The city was full of such places. But everywhere that I drove I saw a haunting memory somewhere from my past. This city's past. And me. And it. We don't like it. The City and its geography mean something else to me. Action. Pain. Fun. Horror. A feeling of invincibility. Death. Accidents, Fights. Angst. Angst and shit. Then it all melts on impact.

The Chinese diplomat and the China Doll. I walked up to the side door in the dark driveway. This was the door Delafasio claimed he saw Steverino exit with the rolled-up carpet on his shoulder. It was the same side door that the Chinese diplomat made his little kid stand outside of. Naked. Yeah. When the kid was as young as three years old. He would misbehave or, if he wouldn't eat his chow mein, or whatever, the diplomat would strip the kid, or make him just wear his underwear and march him right outside. Here. Of course, only in the cold or rain. Maybe on nights like this. The kid would cry and cry to come in. I climbed the three steps and stood where the kid would stand, my nose inches from the window. It was dark inside. I imagined Bo Zoup on the inside looking back at me. Did I learn my lesson yet? What lessons have you learn Bo?

This little kid, this toddler was beaten, too. So was the Doll. The Doll was beaten by the diplomat, too. Strict, old school Chinese style – with a bamboo cane. We found out all this dirt in the grand investigation, mostly from interviews with the China Doll's girlfriends – other Chinese women living nearby, or embassy friends or wives. Mister China Doll, Bo Zoup was a real prick. A sick prick, too. But he didn't kill the Doll. Nor did Steverino. Nope.

"Hello?" A tentative voice came from the rear of the Delafasio house. It was a woman's voice.

"Yes, hello," I said back.

"Can…can I help you?"

She was holding a trash bag by her side door steps. It

was Delafasio's wife. Older. Fatter. But, ain't we all. Except me. I don't eat much, and my expression is timeless.

"Ahhh...no ma'am. O'Hanahan, New York Daily News," I said.

God, I'm good. I made that up cold on the spot.

"I am here looking around. We are doing a story on the China Doll murder. You know the killer Steverino Downing is going to be executed soon, and we are going to run a follow-up story when it happens." God, I'm good. It's like I am a puppet, and some genius works the strings sometimes. She'd never recognize me in the dark and from that distance. Collar up. Hat down.

"Oh. Oh!" she plodded down the steps toward her trash cans.

"I hope I didn't scare you. I am just the kind of reporter that needs to...you know...get on the scene. Look around." I rolled my hands in the air to emphasize my point.

"The Chinese man has moved, you know. He's not there anymore."

"So I have been told."

"Moved back to China."

"Yes, ma'am."

"My husband saw the killer that night."

"Mr. Delafasio?"

"Yes." She put the trash in a can.

"Who ya tawken too out heah?" a male voice from behind the door called out.

"The newspapers," she said.

"News...huh?" Delafasio stepped out onto the porch. He wore a white, tank top, undershirt and pajama bottoms. He was fatter, too. Older, too. His jaw hung open as he turned and looked at me. "Da papers?" he muttered.

"Care to make a comment?" I asked, stepping closer.

"Sure, make a comment," the wife said as she climbed

up their steps and went back into the kitchen.

He walked down the steps, never taking his eyes off of me. He was barefoot.

"Make a comment," I repeated.

Got closer. We were a few feet apart, and he stared at my face.

"You ain't with the papers," he muttered.

"No I'm not."

"You're that detective. The detective on the case. The detective that was shot at Grant's Tomb. In da head."

I stared at him. I wanted to shoot him in the face and in the head and be done with this. But we are far from done.

"What do you want from me?"

"I want to tell you this, you lying, sick fuck," I growled. "I am gonna come back and see you again. Soon. I know you lied about the China Doll. And, you only have one good choice now. The witness protection program. You're gonna talk. If you go tell your buddies at the police department or your other buddies at the pizzeria that I was here? They will just kill you. Fast. Because you are a loose end to them. A worthless loose end they can't have hanging in the wind. And if you don't talk? I'll come back here and I'm gonna kill you myself, you fuck."

His eyes were wide, and his fat jaw hung low. His face was wet now from the misty drizzle. He stood there like a Neanderthal, wax dummy in a museum.

"You have no choice. The witness protection program. Get it on your mind. I will be back," I started to turn.

"When?" he mumbled. That was a stupid question, but stupid people say stupid things when stupefied.

I gave him a .38 caliber stare. Then, I continued my turn and walked out of the driveway. I knew I was walking away into the dark. Into the rain. I didn't plan it that way. Sometimes I scare myself.

"Buuuugger-bear?" the wife called from the kitchen.

I walked down the street and got into my car, feeling all kinds of freestyle charismatic, but then a funny feeling came over me. That didn't go well. That wasn't planned, wasn't controlled and happened by chance. Not good. Not good. I screwed up. Now I didn't know what was at play. What would Delafasio do? And when? I screwed up. Could I even get him on a witness protection program? Sad probably could.

I had planned on hitting a hotel over the GW Bridge in Fort Lee, but really, what would I do there? Stand in the middle of the room and stare at a wall all night? Look at a furniture painting until it went six kinds of blurry and shape-shifted into Beowulf? I got in my car, and I took my hat off and dropped it on the passenger seat. I'm in. Something told me to sit on the house, because I screwed up, and something told me to wait right there. I'd give it three maybe four hours, going over the options in my mind.

Delafasio goes to bed.

Delafasio calls the Five Apes.

Delafasio calls the Mob.

He drives to meet them tonight.

They drive here to meet him tonight.

They pick him up, talk to him and kill him tonight.

They meet tomorrow, take him somewhere and kill him.

They use him to lure me into a trap.

Delafasio keeps our meeting a secret. Option nine, Delafasio lives. Options one through eight he's dumped at a mink farm or in a pigsty and becomes a fatty, food delicacy.

A woman walked down the street. Dressed nice. Late '20s. She spotted me in the car and automatically veered a few feet away on the sidewalk. It's tough for a woman in the city. Walking these streets. There are women walking alone all over the city. All kinds of hours. They are carrying their work bag, or a bag of groceries, or a bag of clothes, grabbed on that last shopping stop after the train or the bus, and on the final walk home. All hours. Veering in and out and away from corners, alleys, men hanging out. Men walking. Men in cars. Veering away their whole way home. I suddenly found myself making the sign of the cross with my fingers. May they all be safe, Jesus.

I thought. Wait! Jesus? Hey, what? The sign of the cross? What am I? Back in Catholic school? Where in hell did that come from? Me and the Holy Trinity ain't had lunch in a long time. And the last time I gagged on a mustard seed.

One hour passed. I sat. A cat-on-a-tonic stakeout. A Cadillac pulled up in front of Delafasio's house. Two guys got out. Both in overcoats and hats. They looked around, but I was a ways up the street. And the light drizzle on the windshield gave me more cover. They were overweight, white guys, tugging on their hats, scarves and coats for the perfect fit on their misshapen bodies. A tailor can't fix what problems you really got, boys. They walked up the stairs and rang the doorbell.

Delafasio answered, and the son of a bitch was fully dressed. No more holey, gravy-stained tank top, underwear shirt. He was ready to go. Sugar-bugger chose option three or four and called the bad guys right after I left the alley. Delafasio didn't stand at the door to talk to them. They were on a mission. All three walked down the stairs toward the car. All three with their heads on a swivel. Delafasio got in the front passenger seat. The guys got in, started the car and drove off.

Stupid fuck. He's a dead man riding. I let them make a turn, and I started my car and hit the gas. When I reached the corner, I could see their car down the avenue, and I was back in the old business. Tailing a car. Hard to do with one car, but I've done it at least 50 times? More.

We drove uptown for a while in the light traffic past Yankee Stadium, down a few side streets and they found the one they liked. A two-lane, one-way street. They pulled over in front of a coffee shop crunched into a row of first floor businesses and upstairs apartments. Two thugs stood outside the door shuffling their feet and talking, making this no ordinary late-night, latte club. The sign above the door read, Cafe Bravo, in red, neon script. All three got out of the car and walked in. One guy, like a valet, got behind the wheel and drove the car down the street to a parking space. I drove by at a normal speed, head forward, but eyes cut to the right so far it hurt, to peek inside. I was good for only one pass on this place. The valet-slash-thug parked the car down the street near the corner, ahead of me. I drove by him. No eye contact.

Down on the corner there was an open "candy store" – like a little, neighborhood grocery store, no doubt run by a guy with 16 kinds of DNA from the Balkans with an added twist of Algeria. I thought about a quick Coke or some coffee, but you have to be careful about these joints down the streets from Mob hangouts. They are on the payroll and will call in any suspicious people they see lingering about. People that is, like me. Out of place. New. Killing time. Not in the hood. So, I had to make myself busy running up and down the avenue, making a plan.

I did however get a parking spot in a few minutes where I could at least spy on their parked car. I imagined the conversation inside the Bravo brew house. In a plush back room, Delafasio would stand there like a child before the high school principle and report that yours truly – old Detective Rusty – was just in his alleyway, telling him I knew he was a liar. I guess he would be stupid enough to report that I had offered him the infamous witness protection program. This term, like a cross of Jesus to Dracula, would net him a death sentence. A bullet to his head. Would he tell them? Be that stupid? Probably. If so, my only question was, would they kill him tonight? Or use him to trap me into some secluded meeting where they would kill the both of us? Would they call the Five Apes in on this? The Five Apes must be stewing about the complete and utter disappearance of their three detectives. They want answers, and they know I've got them. But, knowing the Mob like I do, they may also shut the whole thing down quietly right now. Tonight. And they probably would never bother Julian Managos in Vermont. After all, how could I possibly know about Managos? I knew about the witness. I knew the witness.

I reached into a paper bag in the back seat and grabbed the pack of cigarettes I bought, then fingered around for the matches. I don't smoke, except for the occasional crack pipe, you understand. You see, in New York you can't smoke anywhere anymore, except on an empty freighter on the Hudson on a windy night blowing out to the Atlantic. Your wife, your boss, the restaurant manager, the store owner, the Mayor, King Tut, hippies, whoever, kicks you out into the street to smoke. At any given time, you can find a smoker puffing away, shuffling feet, in all kinds of weather, feeding his or her disgusting habit, on the streets of New York. Outdoor smokers are no longer suspicious. Neither would I be as I stepped from the car, threw on the hat, and threw up the collar and lit the cigarette. It was still drizzling, so I put my back to an apartment brick wall just under a ledge overhang and pretended to smoke, within full view of the Café Bravo street in question.

It all looked normal as streets go. A quiet night in Mafia-town. In this foggy rain, pretending to smoke, I realized that I was a double, dead man. I was a dead man now, too. The renegade cop with an itch, a crazy vendetta. Dead from the cops and now dead from the Mob. Making waves. I almost inhaled a lung full. What did it matter if my rusty lungs took in a little smoke?

Then, one of the door guys started walking up the street. To me? I fake-puffed away, my head tilted to the sidewalk, but my eyes strained and maintained on the street. I had my pistol in my jacket pocket, and I would blow a hole in this fine leather if I had to, to blow a hole into his woolen jacket about, oh, heart high.

But what I saw next was not good news for Delafasio, nor was it really good news for me either because it meant a very complicated night. The guy stopped at the goon's parked, escort sedan. He bent over behind the back of the car. I inched forward to try and see more. I heard some metal fall on the street. A tinny sound – the sound that a dropped license plate makes. He was changing the license plate on the car. Delafasio was a dead man and that would mean tonight. The final drive in untraceable plates. How and where would this happen? I got back in my car as the doorman walked back to the café. I was able to double park near where I had been smoking, because traffic was light.

I saw them. The two goons and Delafasio appeared on the street. A goon playfully shoved a doorman, but he was actually setting the stage for violence. At times when the Mob gets real friendly, things get real dangerous. Like giving you a Coke right before they shoot you. Here, they were setting the "all's well," we are relaxed and relieved, happy signal to Delafasio. No worries. No stress. They climbed in the car, Delafasio in the front passenger seat. It's just the way the boys set it up. They drove off, toward me at first. I lay over in my front seat. As soon as I could, I started my car and crept after them.

Now what happens next and what am I going to do?

CHAPTER 19
GOT MY MIND ON MY MURDER
AND MY MURDER ON MY MIND

For some reason, gunfire in gunfights never hurts my ears. Nor does murder. Not much. Not really. Yet, it hurt me at the gun range when I was calm and my naked ears are unprotected and someone shot a gun. I am not alone in this. Some people say it may have something to do with adrenaline. I don't know. And anyway, murder was on my mind as we drove down the damp streets. Gunshots on my mind. If they took Delafasio back to his house, I would be shocked.

We headed west and then south on Riverside Drive, hugging the Hudson River. Then they took a few smaller forks in the road down west toward the Hudson River waterfront. Not a good direction for my future witness. This spells isolation and dirty deeds. What excuse did they give Delafasio for driving him to the waterfront? Maybe one more key meeting with a key player? They pulled up beside a small dock of some expensive boats and then some not so expensive ones, like work boats. It was Sunday night quiet, late and badly lit. I parked a distance away above them and quietly slipped out of the car.

The three got out of the sedan. I could see Delafasio flinch and stalk about. I think the jerk was now getting the picture, and he ain't in the picture, if you get my drift. One of his gumbas stepped up real close to him. Closer than normal. Closer than natural. I could see this through the patch of woods, a narrow service road, and the few walkways between us. All on a downgrade to the river. I started cutting through these "city woods" to get closer.

Out on the Hudson, a small boat chugged through the black water toward the marina. The way the men positioned themselves, they were awaiting this boat. Delafasio didn't position himself. He was positioned. There was still a light mist in the night air, as the ship's only passenger, the captain, stepped out to the side. He wore a little sea hat and everything. You know, one of those skipper hats. Was there a Gilligan aboard? One goon waved at him. Skipper tossed him a rope, and the goon tied it off on a dock. The other goon had his hand now on Delafasio's elbow. This was rapidly becoming an episode of Lost at Sea. Skipper jumped onto the dock.

I was at a trot now, and I left the tree line, I watched them greet the skipper. Skipper paid no attention to Delafasio. No handshake there, like with the two others. No face-to-face look. Best not to know anything about the body you are about to dump in the Atlantic. When the skipper turned to walk back to his boat, both boys grabbed my boy by the arms and started hauling him down the dock.

Now at a dead run, gun out and up with one hand, not two hands – you run better that way – my shoes hit the asphalt service road and made some noise. Skipper heard me and turned. I shot him. Two to the chest. He just stood there shocked. Damn 9's. Then, I next shot the fat fuck closest to me and to the right of Delafasio. His expensive coat ruffled with the shock, and he fumbled at his pocket. One more to the head in case he got into that pocket. On the dock, the skipper dropped to his knees, babbling, shocked He was saying something, but those words were lost for all eternity. The other shot guy dropped to his knees. He didn't even turn to see me.

It started to look like a seaside prayer meeting until the third guy backed away from Delafasio and started to run off. Big heavy guy in an overcoat and hat. I gave chase. I had to shoot him down soon because the further he ran, the further I would have to haul his blubbery carcass back to the dock. But he tripped on his own and fell like a big tub of guts.

On his back he looked up at me as I ran up to him.

"Rusty?" he said, with his gloved hand up as if it would stop my bullet. "Rusty!"

You know what I saw at this moment? A flash. Yeah like a news flash. All I saw was a girl named Linda Lampert. A high school yearbook photo of Linda Lampert. You see, this punk on the ground was Phillip Fallchey, better known as "Philly 7s" from Little Italy. The Seven's nickname come from carrying a little league baseball bat inside his deep pants pocket and under his jacket. He would beat people with this bat for a variety of business reasons. Homerun swings and in honor of Mickey Mantle and the Mick's Yankee Number 7, Phillip was christened as "Philly 7." Years ago, as a fun pastime, Philly and some friends would set up phony drug deals with rich kids, then rip them off. One night they scammed some college kids at NYU into a marijuana buy at an apartment. The drugs would be delivered to the marks. They robbed them and got rough with them. Linda Lambert and another girl were raped. But Linda was also beaten, and she died in the county hospital. A case was never made, or witnesses were threatened? I don't know. I was a patrolman back then and responded to the scene at the apartment. But, everyone on the street knew the score. It was Philly 7 and his friends. Linda was a freshman in college from western PA. The Daily News and The Post ran pictures of her yearbook photo in the papers. Years later, when working Organized Crime, I met Philly several times, in the course of doing business. I never let on I knew about the rape and murder. I played it straight like a professional.

"Philly 7," I said.

"What the...whatcha doing here? I mean...what..."

"You know what I am doing here. You have been talking about me all night." Jeez, I could smell the cologne wafting off this jerk as I stood over him. I don't know what kind, but it was expensive, and no doubt stolen, because these guys...these guys are human parasites. Real meat eaters. They live off stealing like the rest of us breathe air.

"What's wrong wit you? Cancha leave well enough alone for Christ sakes and now you...you just popped Ronny and, and..."

"The skipper."

"Can you leave me outta this? Looka, looka, I'm running away. Take da stoolie. Can you leave me be? For old time sakes?"

"Philly, you and me? We ain't got no old-time sakes." Isn't this just like a Mob guy? Quoting a Mob movie. We would hear them do this on wiretaps all the time. Art becomes life. Life becomes art.

And now, the end of life. My gunshot cracked across the marina and rolled out over the Hudson. It probably broke the Sunday night silence on up to the Drive and maybe rocketed off a building or two, even in the damp air. Maybe somebody heard the shot? Maybe not. Maybe it sounded like a backfire to them, or a freighter bumping a tug for a push? Or an empty metal truck driving over a pothole. I don't know. But to me? To me, it sounded bittersweet. Like cracking the sweet whip of justice. Linda.

Delafasio scrambled up to me, gasping for air and moaning and making gibberish. Big moron. I would have loved to put my gun up to his temple and send a nine into his skull to bounce around his moron brain.

"You know? Shut up," I said. "I just saved your life…"

"I know! I know!"

"…and you are mine now, you Neanderthal, piece of shit. We've got work to do. Grab this lard ass here and pull him down to the boat."

I jogged over to two dead guys. The skipper was on his back, but still alive. He tried to speak to me, but his lungs were red and wet. His hand shook in the air.

"Yeah, yeah. I know. You want help. I know."

I grabbed him and dumped him over into his boat. Then I grabbed the other dead guy by his lapels and drug him to the boat. Legs. Torso. Arms. Into the boat. Delafasio came up with Philly 7. I searched Philly. Got a pistol, a blackjack and his car keys from his pockets. Money, too. I stuffed the wad of cash into my pocket. Then, together, we rolled him aboard.

"Get in the boat," I told him. "Stay low. If the cops come, just lay down."

I took a quick jog around the docks. There was a small fishing boat I thought I could fire up. I jumped in and looked at the dash. With my knife and flashlight, I hot-wired the thing. It had a tank of gas. I stuck the knife in the ignition and, with a twist, cranked the engine. I untied the boat and brought it around to the skipper's bigger craft. I pulled it to the dock, got out and tied it to the bigger boat. Delafasio just watched in awe – if indeed the state of awe could be achieved by this lizard man. He was shaking from the cold or just from the moment.

I ran to their sedan for a quick look. Nothing inside. I popped the truck. I saw a shovel, a saw, a big pipe and the infamous baseball bat. And a shotgun. I took the shotgun and set it by the dock and got in the car and drove it to the small marina parking lot, where it looked more normal. Next, I jogged up to my car. I wanted to move it further from this area, in case the cops did come, my car wouldn't be found inside an area of investigation, some taped off area not roped off in a lot or something. When I ran back to the boats, I tried to look for my spent shells but couldn't find them. If I played this right, it wouldn't matter anyway. I picked up the shotgun and got into the skipper's boat.

The key to the boat was still in the ignition. I started the engine, and my little fleet backed out of the dock. Two live guys. Three dead guys. Two boats. Was the skipper dead yet? I thought so. Out to the middle of the Hudson we went. Very few boat lights on the river.

"This was the route they'd planned for you Delafasio."

He remained silent.

"When we are through with this, we are picking up your wife and we are leaving New York. You are now my witnesses. You will now try to undo the damage your lies have done. Time for a little redemption."

"Redemption," he repeated.

"Not many find redemption, Delafasio. You have a path to it."

To the right of me? The Statue of Liberty. All lit up. A sight to see, anytime, day or night, even during a murder cover up. Did she see me do my deeds tonight down by the riverside? Will I ever lay down my sword and shield, down by the riverside?

The night air got colder as we bounced on the small waves out into the Atlantic, the lights of Manhattan and Jersey to our rear. Maybe 40 minutes out we went. I shut her down to an idle and, with another rope, tied all the bodies to the captain's chair which was bolted to the deck. I took out my knife and, one at a time, cut open the stomachs of the three men. Grizzly bear work for sure, but necessary. Dipshit just stood there shocked.

"Get in the other boat."

Delafasio pulled the smaller boat we'd been towing up alongside and slipped in. I handed him the shotgun. I got a smaller piece of rope and tied off the steering wheel to one position. Then I increased the throttle to an easy but steady speed. I joined Delafasio in the smaller boat as he held it tight to the big ship for me. Yeah, I got a little wet. Actually, I got a lot wet. But murder is a wet business. A knife twist started the engine up again. I untied the boats, then I turned the throttle up so I could run up beside the big boat.

"Hand me that shotgun."

I got it and took aim at the waterline of the boat. I shot it once. Now she would be taking in some water. Then I shot a little higher. Then shot a little higher again. Now this boat would run itself out into the Atlantic, straight for France, until it ran out of gas, or sank first. And if all worked to plan, the boat and the three stooges would disappear forever into the ocean. And the Mob wouldn't know what happened to Delafasio either. I threw the shotgun into the drink. I even tossed my new pistol out there, too. There are other guns, better guns to use than the ones with ballistics tied to three murders, just in case Moe, Larry and Curly gestate to the surface. But they shouldn't. That's what the knife work was for.

The Atlantic Ocean is a great accomplice for murder. From Boston, to New York, the Jersey shore on down to Miami, the Mob has dropped bodies and guns off in her and even used her for fast escapes. Lakes and rivers can be, too. Either way, a real slaughter-hand in the killing business will take a body out there and slit the belly good. It is usually the stomach and gases that ferment and decay that, over time, swell the torso and float ol' Lefty Louie to the surface. Cut that gut open, and you can prevent that. Another thing they'll do, if the weather is right, is they'll do this little gutting operation right in the water with them, right next to the boat. Strip down and get right to the wet work. This way there is little evidence found on dry land or in a boat, should one be found and tested. Not all boats are sunk like this one. I made a case once on some victim's blood that had gotten on the side of a boat and into the rope of an anchor. I had good intel that a real estate agent was killed and disposed of like this, next to a boat in waist deep water off the shore of Staten Island. So we checked the whole length of the anchor rope of the suspect's boat. Inside the course fiber of the anchor rope we found the victim's blood.

We ran our little boat back up the Hudson with Miss Liberty now to our left. We didn't speak. What's to say? I made several passes by the marina and saw it was as quiet as when we left. I docked the boat in its bay. The owner had his boat back sans a little gas. Well, that and with a few modifications on his electrical system. I felt relieved and actually a little tired for a change. A little, happy-tired. My brain really felt clear though. Maybe it was the saltwater air? I half-way expected to see ol' General Grant sitting calmly on the dock waiting for me. He wasn't there.

We trudged silently back to my car. The Delafasio evacuation was next in the lineup.

"Call your wife and tell her to pack for a fast trip. Don't explain," I ordered as we sat in my car. I handed him my phone. I tapped the phone with my finger and repeated, "Don't explain."

And, no. My ears didn't hurt from those gunshots.

CHAPTER 20
OUTSIDE IN, INSIDE OUT

Southbound on the New Jersey Turnpike. Not a good idea to ride the Turnpike after you've killed a lot of people, you know. Rental car or not. Cameras coming and going. They catch license plates. Photos of drivers. Times in. Times out. But no case followed me southbound. I did a good enough job covering up so far. No one should be looking for us, our car or our plates. Or my mug. Still, I will exit the Turnpike before Agnes' closest exit. See if anyone's behind me. Take the back roads. The location of Agnes' house is top secret.

I have two silent statues in the back seat. They may as well have been dead. Mr. and Mrs. Delafasio. Mrs. Delafasio was steaming mad at Mr. Delafasio. She now knew the whole story of his so-called witnessing. My surprise appearance in their driveway six hours ago has turned their whole world completely upside down. I do that to people sometimes. Selling crack or even back in the NYPD, you didn't want me showing up in your life. I mean, patrol officers are not life changers, but when you work homicide and organized crime? Your appearance can be bone-rattling when you show up.

Delafasio was now my accomplice in three murders, too. But in a way they were all in self-defense, weren't they? In a way. In the big picture, anyway. Real police would have stopped Delafasio's murder and arrested the three guys on the dock. But, the Five Apes would have eventually shown up. The charges would have been lame and dropped on me so I could disappear from the system. Into their system. Then they would have caught me and tortured me and killed me. But I'm not the real police, am I? I am the Faux Police. The Anti-Police.

Right then, working out these details, I got a screwy worm in my head. A cloud fell inside my skull all of a sudden. Like my brain had a bath in a bad flavor or a sickly sensation. Not good. This is not good. I tried to concentrate on the road. But my throat started to close up, too. The windpipe shrank to a thin straw. I tried to breathe and breathe deep. Shake it off. Shake it off! Get a grip! Drive!

But I couldn't drive. I pulled on the steering wheel and got the car off the road. I unclicked and threw off the seat belt. Opened the door and cop-shoved it out further open with a push of my foot. It was like I was going to throw up, but throw up what? My brain? I got outside the car and rain hit my face. I stepped to the front of the car and leaned back on the hood. I think I groaned a bit. Weird grunting of a man losing his mind. Like an animal. Was I going to black out? Right here on the Jersey Turnpike? Pass out and die?

Cars and a truck blew by me. It was cold. I lost myself in the bouncing and rolling lights, frozen. Then…then, it was better. Better. And better. My guts slid back down where they belonged like I was swallowing a big lump of un-chewed food. I coughed up some phlegm. Was this a simple, what they call a panic attack? If it was? It sucked. It sucked bad. I walked back to the car door and got inside. The Delafasios were wide-eyed and stone quiet.

"Yeah, yeah, I know. Your life rests in the unholy hands of a spaz."

"Do you want me to drive?" Mr. Delafasio asked.

"Driving is the least of my problems," I said as I edged the car back onto the highway. "Right now I'd kill for some strawberry ice cream." I wasn't kidding. Doesn't that sound just great?

******

I slept until 3 p.m. the next day. We got to Agnes' at 3 a.m., and had to settle down and settle them in. Agnes took it all in stride. In her robe and giant slippers, she guided the Delafasios to a bed. I called Sad right away on our disposable phones, which I still did not completely trust, woke her up and tried to fill her in, as cryptically as possible, on the new developments. I felt like I was calling my old Captain, updating him on breaking news on a midnight call-out. Captain Kuzman. Nice guy. A real lush, but nice. That was like the last time I checked in on my progress in the middle of the night. To Kuzman.

I sat upright in bed in my little room filled with knick-knacks and old books. It was time for a Zulu pill, and I got one from the bottle on the dresser and gulped it down dry. I needed those little bastards to think straight. I got dressed in a sweatshirt and jeans and decided to see who-was-what-where in the serene home of Agnes. I could hear quite a bit of talking and noise downstairs.

I walked barefoot down the steps, and the whole first floor was like a booming business office. I mean, people I didn't know were there typing on laptops, talking on cell phones in the living room and dining room. Lamont, the guard, was there. Standing. Guarding. I walked by him.

"I hope no one was followed?" I said to him.

They all ignored me as I walked through the living room and into the kitchen. The Delafasios where seated at the big kitchen table. Sad was with them, her hands folded on the table. A bald, fat man with a laptop sat with them, clacking away. He was taking Delafasio's statement. Mrs. Delafasio smiled at me. I think she was beginning to understand my part in this three-act play. Peter came through and hit me on my triceps. Agnes was doing dishes.

"Cawfee, Russ?" Agnes asked.

"Ah, yes. Thanks. Black."

Agnes handed me a mug.

"Dunkin Donuts on the counter."

I nodded. I got my fingers on a white, sticky powdered special, sure to have a treasure of strawberry jam on the inside. Then I stepped near the stenographer and caught Sad's attention, motioning my head to the left for Sad to meet me in the hallway. She got up, and I followed her there.

"Probably a good idea to skip the three killings last night in the final report?" I whispered.

"Mr. Delafasio fully understands you saved his life last night and knows what he is doing now will save his life in the future. We will not include those events in this or any statement to appeal the Downing conviction. As your counsel…"

"My counsel?"

"As your counsel, I will refrain from admitting any damaging information about you. The record shows you simply contacted him and convinced him to tell the truth. And they soon will be off to the Federal Witness Protection Program."

"Then my work here is done, Tonto," I said. I could see she didn't know who in hell Tonto was.

"No, it's not." She touched my arm and then went back to the kitchen table. But I felt like I was done. What's next for me? Should I start setting up my next coke deal? Or what?

The afternoon passed, and the appeal work started slowing down. Some workers left with Lamont in a big van. Agnes cooked a big pot roast which was to die for, as they say. Scrumptious.

At 7:30 p.m., two black Suburbans pulled up. Marshals came in. They, of course, knew Sad. They methodically spoke with the Delafasios and collected up what things they threw together from last night. Before they walked out the side door, Mr. Delafasio stopped and turned to look at me. Me. Their blessing and their curse. Me. He half-smiled, half-grimaced and nodded a goodbye. I nodded back. I still don't like the jack-off. Mrs. Delafasio stepped in pace right behind him. She smiled and waved at me. Mrs. Jack-Off.

With the winter-weather sun set. I gathered all my clothes and shoes from the night before. I knew I had to destroy them. Agnes had a metal barrel in the middle of the backyard, obviously for burning trash. How hot could I make that bad boy? Armed with some fireplace matches and lighter fluid, I took them all out to the yard, threw some logs into the barrel, splashed it all and flicked in the lit match. A blanket of smelly heat and yellow light rolled across my face.

I heard the back screen door open and shut and heels on the wooden porch steps. It was Sad. She walked up to my little funeral pyre.

"Burning these clothes. You never know. You never know about things like blood spatter," I said. I shoved them down into the barrel with a thin metal pipe.

"You are very thorough."

"I know my way around a murder."

"Yes."

I stirred my destruction of evidence.

"So, have I become your hit man?"

"No, Rusty. You haven't."

There was an uncomfortable silence. Just the cracking and snaps of the fire. I looked up at her face, her afro, ringed in a red glow. Behind her were the flatlands of New Jersey. Grassland. Some trees. I half expected to see a giraffe walking back there behind her. She had that mystique of turning everywhere she went into someplace else.

"You're a witch," I blurted out. Call it a problem with impulse control.

Her head shifted side to side, and she sighed.

"Rusty, sometimes things get so confusing. So obtuse. So big. The rules…the laws, get so big that nothing can get accomplished from within. You see, this I know, but you don't see this like I have, from several countries."

"South Africa," I mumbled, poking the fire.

"Yes. Other places, too. Bosnia. Russia. You have no idea what it's like to be embedded in those worlds day to day. Inside. Or worse, these poor people inside the jail of these despots. You think you do, but you don't. Your view of the world is distinctly American. In these horrible places, nothing changes. Nothing gets done inside their rules."

"These…obtuse…rules."

"Some things must happen from the outside in order to straighten things inside out. Your country is not immune from these problems and these types of solutions." She folded her arms and looked off over this New Jersey savannah. "You have the Five Apes, or any bad cops, like the old Rampart scandal in LAPD. You have the Mafia. You have politicians that…"

"Yeah," I interrupted the depressing dirge.

"There is no real justice sometimes. And, justice comes in many forms," she continued.

I poked the fire. I could still see one shoe in there,

bubbling and cracking.

"So, what do you want of me? Cure me? Get me killed? Am I a lab rat, or just a rat on a leash?" I asked.

"I let you go to Vermont and to New York, on your own…I sent you…because…because we needed something to happen. Something crazy. Sometimes something crazy has to happen. But I trusted you. I trusted that you wouldn't be too crazy. You were as cold and calculating as I anticipated, like you were at the doctor's office when we were attacked. And that night afterward. Peter thinks so, too. Like a soldier. Better than a soldier because you know the law. In two short days you have changed everything about this case. It is rogue. Just turning you loose.

"So far, with the shock treatments and the medications, you have been highly functional. There is a highly functioning part of your brain at work, and other parts of your brain have been healing. That night under the George Washington Bridge, when that man told you about the China Doll murder, your brain had healed to the point that his message affected you. Affected the old Rusty in you. The healing Rusty. A sense of justice arose. Swelled up. Empathy. A conscious…"

"They are overrated."

"…and then, I am afraid, that parts of your brain will never heal. But, parts of your brain will learn to compensate for those parts."

"And that is the Sesame Street version of neuroscience."

"I think I have a job for you, at my foundation," she said, bluntly.

"A job," I mumbled. Now that scared me.

"I work with Amnesty International, our DNA Freedom Science Foundation, and so many causes. Worldwide. Not just here in the United States. So many times we need someone from the outside drilling in."

"Shooting in."

"Drilling in. Someone…"

"With weird, unhealed brain parts."

"…someone with unusual solutions and a lot of experience. Instinct. Someone…fearless."

"Another overrated trait."

FINALLY, that shoe curled up into a bright red heap. It smelled funny, like poison gas.

"Rusty, we will continue to treat you, and I want you to come to work for me. You are utterly unique; and I need someone like you. You will have an office. A car. A home even."

"What about major medical?"

"That, too."

I was only joking.

"I don't think a guy with a hole in his head is insurable. Why not just use your commando friend, Peter, to do all of this fearless work?"

"I do. But Peter is not quite like you."

"I'm crazy."

"You…are crazy. And my job is to keep you a little crazy." She said that with half a smile.

Creepy. Was that a joke?

"Thanks, Doctor Moreau."

"Thursday morning you'll have another shock treatment. Every time we do these, we run the risk of you coming down with temporary amnesia or other problems, but you show no pathology for this problem yet. Are you experiencing anything physically or mentally unusual?"

I laughed, but I really wanted to cry, then laugh about the crying. How's that for an answer?

"Sad, I have no words to describe how I think or what I feel. It ain't right. I know that much."

We stood in silence. A neighbor's dog bayed down the road. She looked at me. I looked at the fire.

"I will submit the Delafasio statement to the Governor of Connecticut and petition for a new trial tomorrow afternoon. As you know, if a witness recounts his or her testimony in a murder case, however crucial, this does not automatically throw the case out. Lots of witnesses recant their testimony at this point. Lots of governors ignore that. Lots of people are still executed rather than having their sentences reversed or even a temporary stay granted."

I nodded.

"But still Rusty, you did good. Really good."

"You recall...I killed numerous people."

"And those people you killed were murdering criminals. They are the same all over the world. No different. I cannot openly condone the crime of killing, but this is a war."

War. And I didn't know what to say to that. A raped, South African brain surgeon talking about a world war on injustice, all in a south Jersey backyard owned by a lady names Agnes who was involved with Sad. Why? Was Sad doing something trying to redeem herself? And from what?

Redemption. Where is that? Is there anything I can do to redeem myself for what I have done to people? Innocent people. I still had the driver license in my wallet of the man I killed for his ID. I opened the wallet and pulled it out. I tossed the D.L. into the fire. It curled up and vanished. Just like that poor guy did. My God, my God, what have I done?

"You want the job?" Sad's head tilted forward, and her eyes widened.

"What's the job title?"

"Human Resources Specialist. That way, no one will know what you do, and you can do anything for us under such a job title."

"Yeah, I'll take it. I've apparently got nothing else to do after I burn this last shoe."

"Good. You will be closely supervised. Especially at

first. You understand this."

"Yeah."

"Day and night for a while."

"Yeah."

We stood there.

"Sad, you have no idea what I have done to people these last few years, since…since they turned me loose from the hospital."

"I can't imagine what you've done. And I don't want to know unless there is a psychological need-to-know. But, if you feel guilt? If you feel guilty? That is a positive thing."

"Yeah, well. I do. I feel a lot of guilt. Oh, and I also need a new gun."

CHAPTER 21
NOTHING BUT ME AND
A BULLET IN MY HEAD

I was more than perfectly content.

Agnes was driving me home...home? Listen to me... driving me back to her house after my latest shock treatment. I was utterly melted into the front seat of her Toyota. Relaxed. I was a little numb. A little veneer of something seemed to cover my scalp, but I didn't care. A restfulness settled deep in my lungs. Like a sustained "ten deep breaths" feeling. Bliss. A dumb bliss. Everything looked a little clearer, too. Bigger. Like a larger movie screen. How else can I describe this? Okay. Ever stand in front of about 15 big screen TVs in an electronics store? Each screen looks fine, but when you get to looking at each one of them, some screens have a better, clearer image? Some look better than others? Right then, the world was a bigger, clearer TV picture to me. What a day. What a day. What a day.

Agnes had her seat pulled all the way to the steering wheel which, compared to her, looked like the wheel of a semi-truck. Her elbows stuck out wide. She had acted a little pissed today, kind of a little put-out about this chore of driving me and was rather quiet going and now quiet coming back. We'd been to a small clinic in Newtown, PA. A wounded Dr. Suliman presided once again, over the scorching of my brains. In a back room of the joint he lit me up like a Christmas tree. And, no, I did not recognize him again, but he did show me how his gunshot wound was healing, so it must have been him.

"Thanks for taking me, Agnes." I thought I'd better say it.

"You are welcome."

"So, how did Sad help you out? How do you know her?"

She grimaced a bit, enough to move her pug nose around. "She got me out of jail."

"Oh," I looked at her gremlin-like profile, expecting a follow-up, but none came.

"Bonded you out, or…"

"No, she got me out of the state penitentiary."

"The state pen. For what?"

"Murder."

"Murder?"

"Murder."

"Who ja kill?"

"My son."

I nodded my head, and looked up the road ahead, digesting that one. Not many mothers kill their sons. Once in a while, crazy sons kill their mothers…so…you know…Wow!

"Did you really kill him?" I said, expecting Sad to have freed her because she was innocent.

"Yeah."

"Then how did Sad get you out?"

Silence.

"We need a few things from Sam's," she said, pulling off the road and onto a shopping center parking lot.

We parked and got out and, for the first time in a very long time, I entered a Sam's Wholesale Club. We must have made an odd pair. Agnes was odd enough by herself, but the two us together? The flaming matchstick and the imp fairy. She led the way, and I pushed the shopping cart. I remembered I used to stop by the books for a bit while my wife shopped. The girls would stop too, looking over the kid's books and DVDs. Agnes saw me slow down and rubber-neck that book section.

"Go ahead," she said, and she took over the cart.

Almost with hesitation, I wandered over to the rows of books. I looked over the covers. Who were these authors? I know that Sam's always carried the "sheeple" books – hey, my old nickname for the mass paperback book trade came right back to me – for the common books thrust on the sheep-people readers, those who mindlessly pick up the 12th or 33rd thriller from the same tired author who probably has a fleet of ghost writers at his disposal. The books are too long and boring to be a single TV episode and too long and boring to be a movie.

Then I spotted an oversized paperback about a guy's life story in the Siberian, Russian Mafia. True story. Now that was different. I thumbed through it. Hmmmm, maybe I'll steal it? It's awful big though. First thought in my criminal mind. Then I remembered. I still had hundreds of dollars in my wallet. I didn't need to steal anything. I grabbed the book. I walked to the aisle's end, looking for Nancy, I mean Agnes. I glanced down the aisle of kid's book. It was empty. Just a gray cement floor where kids would be. Should be. And for a second, I didn't want to leave. I knew why.

Nothing much had changed at Sam's since I was there last. Nothing but me, and the fact that a bullet had passed through my head and taken part of my brain along with it.

"Get a book?" It was Agnes. Her cart was full of canned food and meat.

"Yes, I did. I have some money today. I'll pay for all this?"

"Sure! I got a lot of food. Since you showed up, we've been throwing some real, large parties. Oh, let's get some tortilla chips."

We got two kinds of chips. No telling how long I would be "stationed" with Agnes. I gave her two, one hundred-dollar bills. While she checked out, I looked at all the big screen TVs, checking my vision, checking the various perceptions of life though my looking glass. Clear, fuzzy, fuzzier. Static. Like the phases I see in life now.

Done, then we rolled out onto the lot, loaded the car, and we were back on the road again.

"Ten years ago, I killed my son," she said.

I thought we were through with that dreaded conversation and, due to my spacey attitude, I had forgotten all about the subject.

"He was always a problem child," she continued. "But, he got married to a very nice girl. Barbara. She was so nice. From the neighborhood. He got a decent job with the Water Department. "They had a little boy, and he was the apple of my eye…"

Where's this going?

"But my son – Gerald – Gerald was a beater. He was a wife beater, and he used to punch that precious girl. Her mother and father knew it, too. We knew it, and we should have done something about it. Her father was a little Jewish waste, you know, he wouldn't make a peep. He was a man, and he should have done something. What a waste of space. He was so afraid of Gerald. We all shoulda done something. Then one afternoon, I'll never forget, I got a call from the hospital…"

"He'd beat her that bad?" I asked.

"No. Worse, Rusty! He'd beat that little baby boy. Beat him so bad they called an ambulance to their house. Barbara's mother called me from the emergency room. She said the cops were there to investigate and everything. Oh my God. Oh my God, my heart was broken in a second on the phone in my kitchen! Oh, that poor baby. That baby boy, beaten. What if he died? I threw on a coat and went to Hillside General. To the emergency room."

We stopped at a red light, and she continued.

"When I got there, I headed to the emergency room parking lot where I saw them all standing outside on the parking lot. The cops argued with Gerald. His wife. Her parents. It was like a nightmare. And my stupid son was trying to leave! The cops grabbed his arms, and he pulled away from them. Pushed them away, and he started to run away. He ran across the parking lot."

The light turned green, and we drove on.

"Then he saw my car, saw me and started running toward me, waving his arms like, you know, like I was his goddamn getaway car or something. Like he could count on me to drive him away from the police. You know, I saw his face when he saw my face and recognized me. That face. All that long friggin' hair he had and all those tattoos of human skulls. I'd had enough. My foot hit the gas pedal. I hit him. I ran right over him. Enough of him, I said to myself. I ran over his chest, the police said. It killed him."

We turned down her long street.

"It was in this car we're in now. I got out of the car, and I cursed him while he lay there. Cursed him for all the trouble he'd caused me and his father – God rest his father's soul – he died of a heart attack years ago. I cursed him for all he'd done to his little family. The cops all heard this. They heard me gun the car and run it at him. They arrested me, and I confessed. I confessed to the truth. They got a written confession of what happened. I was a real mess."

"No lawyer."

"No lawyer because what was there to hide? And a part of me died on that lot, too."

"And Sad got you out of the pen, reversed the conviction?"

"On an appeal. I was poorly represented. Public defender. And I just threw myself on what they call 'the mercy of the court.' But it's Jersey."

"Jersey."

"Convicted. Ten years. But Sad took the appeal for nothing and tricked them all and got me out! God bless her, too."

"And the baby healed up?" I added, more matter-of-factly than questioning.

She pulled into her driveway, stopped the car and we sat there.

"He died. He died the next night, too."

She looked me in the eyes. "And my heart is broken. Every day I live with this. Is it an eye for an eye? A son for a grandson? I don't know. Is that what it is?"

Eye for an eye. Son for a grandson? That's some biblical shit right there. Whew. She got out of the car. I chose to sit there numb for a few more seconds, and I wasn't that numb from the shock treatment.

We unloaded the car and carried it all inside. I helped her put away the groceries, even opened up the chips and started working on them with some dip. What's on TV? Do I have any slippers here?

Then the phone rang. She answered.

"Russ, it's for you. Sad."

I took the phone, "Yello."

"Rusty, the governor has just denied the appeal and the stay of execution. The clock is still ticking on Downing."

"Then we have no choice. We have to go China."

CHAPTER 22
EASTERN GIRLS LOVE WESTERN EYES

Lamont drove. We blasted up the Turnpike. I had with me a tote bag Agnes fixed for me with a toothbrush, toothpaste, a brush and my new Siberian Mafia book. I had to catch a plane you see. A private jet, actually. Just four weeks ago I was stealing cars and knocking down old ladies for chump change, and now a small jet awaits me, so life is very weird. We exited the turnpike and entered Teterboro Airport, just 12 miles outside Manhattan, but still in Jersey. All the metropolitan New Yorker, bigwigs with jets use Teterboro, and Sad is one of those bigger-wiggers. Lamont drove right onto the tarmac, pulling on our flashers and headlights. We drove up to another car parked by a jet. Sad and Peter got out of that car. We parked near them.

I got out, and what did I see? Hanging on a chain link fence like two monkeys in the Bronx Zoo, about 50 yards away? Two guys in suits, standing right by an unmarked police sedan. I pointed to them.

"You see!"

"We know. They followed us from the Institute," Sad said. "Don't worry. They don't know what we are doing or where you are going."

I stopped and looked at them. They are missing three detectives, and they must know by now their Mob buddies are missing three mooks. And they know we have their witness because Sad filed the execution stay two days ago, alluding to one. "The jig is up," as we used to say.

"Let's go," Sad said, waving me over to the small, private jet. We climbed aboard, and Peter and I sat down in some very plush seats inside. Sad didn't sit. She wasn't coming along.

"Here are your passports. You both sell medical supplies."

She gave them to us. I looked at mine. My new name was Harley Dunnigan.

"Where did you get these?" I asked, tapping my hand with the little blue book in it.

"The state, undercover narcotics man."

Mister Dockers.

"I see. I know how that goes. I hope he's clean." I shoved the ID in my tote bag.

"It's from Stanley. It's okay. You are going to Atlanta, then to South Africa on Delta. Then to Shanghai. Peter has your luggage and your medications. We know right where our man is working. In a medical clinic."

"Why Africa?"

"We are picking up gear and making some contacts," Peter said. "I have an old SAS friend that lives in Shanghai. Does security work there for South African and Chinese businessmen. We will make some connections in Johannesburg and be off to China with some help."

"And the two apes hanging out on the fence?"

"They can't follow this jet. And when they look at the flight plan, it's to DFW in Texas," Sad said.

"Let them follow me to South Africa," Peter added. "I catch them on my turf? They will become dinner for hungry lions."

"Okay." I loved it when he talked all dirty like that.

"How are you feeling?" she asked me.

"Pissed. All around pissed. What do you want us to do in Shanghai, other than the obvious? Contact Bo Zoup?"

"Anything you think you need to do to free our client. Solve the problem, Rusty."

"I see, we'll just open up that fortune cookie when we get there. But I want to kidnap him."

"You watch him," Sad pointed first to Peter, then to me. "And you watch him," Sad pointed to me, then to Peter.

"And you make sure Agnes is safe!" I said, pointing back at her. I predicted someone would successfully follow somebody at some point. Somehow. Somewhere.

"They followed us here, not you Rusty," Sad said as she walked out of the plane.

A tall, skinny flight attendant came in. She had one of those funny uniform hats on. She needs a milkshake. Too skinny.

"Good morning, gentlemen," she said as she pulled the door closed behind Sad and sealed it. She picked up a phone and told the pilot we were good to go. The plane taxied around to the strip, and I saw the two apes still hanging on the fence, drooling. I could see that one wrote down the serial number on the plane. I couldn't recognize them.

"Ever been to Africa, Rusty?"

"No."

"It's a lot like here, only way more dangerous."

"Hmmm."

"Ever been to China?" he asked.

"No."

"Yes, as they say, I have a good friend there. We will be in good hands."

I nodded, buckling my seatbelt.

"Rusty, Zoup is working in a medical building. He is the manager of a company that specializes in a certain type of plastic surgery. I cannot pronounce the Chinese name. They take eastern girl eye lids and alter them into western-shaped eyelids. It is a booming business there. A craze."

"Shang-eye for the Shang-hai. Better than foot binding. Zoup has come a long way. Fallen a long way. From international diplomat to office manager of an eyelid factory."

"Excuse me gentlemen, but after our takeoff, I'll be serving you some beverages. We also have a very nice, hot lunch."

"Fantastic," Peter said to her, then turned back to me. "By the time the Mob murdered his wife, he was pretty much a disgrace in many circles. His government was scandalized just by the murder alone. The Chinese Mafia aggravated. The Triads consider him untrustworthy. Still, he did help push through the trade agreements after the murder. He'd learned enough of a lesson. A bloody lesson. Then Zoup was called back to China to remove him from the mess. But the Triads owed him. 'Owed him a favor' as you Americans would say. They fixed this job for him."

"Prepare for takeoff."

The flight attendant sat down in the front and strapped in. The engine accelerated. Peter leaned over toward me.

"We just learned from Interpol that the Triads gave him this job in the surgery clinic. They collect protection from the business as they control so much of the plastic surgery enterprise in parts of China."

"The Triads," I repeated quietly. I didn't know very much about the Triads. I never worked Chinatown in NYPD. And I never knew much more than some news reports and gossip about them. Wait! Did someone mention a hot lunch?

I sat back in my seat and ate that hot lunch. It was good. I started to read my book, and I was very interested in it. I haven't read a book since, well, before I was shot in the head. We landed in Atlanta, then we were taken by taxi to the main terminals and wasted more time in the international terminal. While waiting to board, I read more. I couldn't stop. We boarded, first class thank you very much, Sad. I continued to read. The Siberian Mafia was vicious! I remembered that I was always interested in organized crime. My dream job was working in O.C. I worked my whole life to get that job. I remembered that when I was a kid, I saw the Mob movie with Charles Bronson called "The Valachi Papers." It was mostly a true story. It was a great movie and, to me, better than "The Godfather" movie. I have to watch that again, I decided. And this book was fascinating. Fascinating to see the similarities and differences between our Mafia and their Commie Mafia. No matter what you call it, dictatorships, Fascism, Communism, the human animal runs on capitalism. Even under Communism, like in Russia, China, Cuba, a second, secret economy, a shadow economy exists, because we all buy, and we all sell. We trade. New York City. Frankfurt. Siberia.

I ate. I slept. I read. I remembered.

******

We landed in Cape Town. Peter rented a car. We drove out of the city. The city and the country scenery were amazing. The coastline was rugged. The savannahs, I guess they call them, great.

"We are going to my parent's house. They own a vineyard," Peter told me.

"So Peter, are you married?"

"No."

"Do you have a main squeeze?" I asked.

He smiled at that.

"A...main squeeze?" he repeated. "Yes, I do. I have a lady friend in New York."

"A lady of a friend. Does she know what you do?"

"More or less," he paused, then, "mostly less."

We looked at each other and both nodded.

Within the hour we were driving down a long, private dirt road through a large vineyard. Hundreds of rows of vines on either side, flicking by like an electric fan. A house that I could see up ahead was white with a copper roof. Behind the house was range of granite looking mountains. I saw some people working, and I thought I saw one running. But, as we got closer, I recognized it as a monkey. A big monkey. A freaking monkey was running ahead us and, when we got even closer, I saw two small, baby monkeys running with it. Peter blew his horn at them as we buzzed by. They ignored us.

"The baboons. The horn will not bother them. Not even the vuvuzela horn scares them. They like the sauvignon blanc grape skins here. A favorite. But they get into the wine at the warehouse, too. Some get drunk and pass out, out here. Others go home at night to the mountains and come back in the mornings. But they are not just eating our grapes, they are raiding our kitchens and ripping the thatch right off the roofs of our sheds. Stealing anything and everything they can haul off. They are becoming increasingly bold and destructive. We cannot even leave a window open in the summer."

Wow. Monkey problems.

Some teenagers on bicycles pedaled past us. They waved. We waved.

"Neighbors," Peter said.

We pulled up in front of the house, got out, and an

elderly couple appeared on the porch. They smiled broadly. It was Mom and Pop. Max and Helen, as they introduced themselves. We carried our luggage in.

"You must be exhausted," Helen said, helping us in. Peter explained that we were just passing through on business, on our way to China.

"Oh dear God, I hope you are not trying to free someone from China!" his mother said.

"Just to talk to a man there, Mum," Peter said.

We had lunch in this plantation style home in a large dining room. The whole house reminded me of a ranch, but different. Africa-different if that makes any sense? They talked family business. They talked shop. Wine shop. Laughed. I said little. I was afraid to speak. Afraid I would spit out something wrong. Afraid to mess up the moment. Afraid I'd say or do something that would make them think I wasn't normal. It seemed I might ruin something. Their moment.

We were exhausted, at least I was. They showed me to my room upstairs. I crashed on the guest bed; the Siberian mobster book open on my chest. Not standing. I awoke horizontal hours later in a sunset world. A magic world. Wind blowing the curtains. Wind chimes. Birds I'd never heard before. Strange, alien. Yet familiar.

I rummaged through my suitcase of surprises that Sad, or somebody, packed for me. I needed a shower, bad. I grabbed some clothes and found the bathroom down the hallway. Shower. Shave. Brush teeth. Pick toenails. Scratch balls. And then barefoot, I walked downstairs.

Peter's father sat in the living room on a couch with charts of some kind on his lap. He pulled his glasses off and smiled at me.

"Come sit over here, Rusty."

I did. Uncomfortable, but I did. I dropped into a large chair across from him.

"Peter tells me you were wounded in the service."

"Yes, I was. Not military. Police. Police service."

He nodded.

"I have been shot. In the chest. In the thigh, too. On the Angola border. Wars too...well, too complicated and small for someone not from here – not from Africa – to even comprehend. Many times, most of us here can't even comprehend them."

I nodded.

"People around the world, Americans too, thought us evil race mongers in those days. But few know that we also greatly feared the Communists. The Commies were entrenched in the black cause. The Russian Commies were everywhere, and we were surrounded by them. There were thousands of Cuban soldiers in Angola supporting the SWAPO. Russian tanks. Russian troops.

"There's a photo up there of Peter and Nelson Mandela. Many of us like Mandela in the end. But those damned Communists! Well, ha, I am sorry to bring up this old news."

"Did Peter grow up here?" I said, turning my head to the wall of pictures. Peter in numerous police and military groups.

"Yes he did. His whole life. Someday I hope he will return here and run this place. But I know he does very important work in New York City."

"Yes he does," I blurted out. "He frees innocent people." I liked the sound of that. Freeing innocent people.

Just then I had the funny feeling that Peter's mom had stepped into a large hallway to the kitchen. Someone was standing there, suddenly, I could sense it way off in the corner of my mind.

"You dirty, son of a filthy bitch!" Peter's dad growled.

Huh? I looked at his face, and he was looking at the hallway, not at me. I turned red. The mother figure in my peripheral vision was a filthy son of...? I turned toward the hallway. There was someone there, alright. But, it wasn't Peter's mother. It was the biggest damn baboon I've ever seen. Baboon-zilla. It was upright but kind of sitting on its haunches. His left hand held a box of breakfast cereal. He had his right hand thrust deep inside the open box, scooping around for a handful. He? She? What...it? It stared toward Max, then looked at me, then back at him, like a bored human, just passing through.

"Helen!" Max cried out.

I didn't know what to do. What do you do with a baboon standing and eating breakfast cereal in your living room? I have heard of people shooting an elephant in their pajamas. But no more Groucho Marx lines came to me as I watched the gorilla stuff handful after handful of cereal into his mouth a few short feet away from where I stood.

"Helen!" Max cried out again sitting forward on his couch.

This monkey was none too happy with all the yelling for Helen. It opened its big mouth. It showed all its long, yellow, Nosferatu teeth. This was like a primal fear night-mare. It howled. Like some idiot, I instinctively howled back, my mouth wide open, too. All my teeth showing, too. Apes aping apes.

The monkey responded by throwing a handful of cereal at me.

Helen appeared, holding a double barrel shotgun. Ap-parently, she recognized the human and primate yelling.

"Get out of here! Get out of here! Get out of here!" she yelled.

"Go! Go! Go!" Max yelled waving his hands.

I ran to the front double doors and opened them wide yelling, "Get out of here, you damn filthy ape!" What would Charlton Heston think about that?

Max and I swung our arms wildly and hollered. Helen aimed the gun. The baboon ran for the open doors, but I was still too close! It made a dash right for me, its head lunging forward and snapping his horror-movie choppers my way. I climbed right back over the chair I was near, and it toppled over backward, with me tumbling right with it. I tried to get back up fast, but I slipped again. By the time I stood, the monkey was out the door standing on the front yard, still with the cereal box clutched and dented in its hands.

"Get away and stay away!" Helen shouted. She fired that shotgun, both barrels into the air. The monkey jumped a foot straight up with sheer shock, screamed and ran off into the vineyard. The couple watched.

"The arrogance of that bastard," Max said.

"The…" and then Helen suddenly broke out into a fit of laughter. She doubled over and had to set the shotgun down by a porch chair. It became a harder laughter. Max started to laugh, too. He laughed out loud. I don't know if they were laughing at me because I'd made a monkey face right back at the baboon and screeched out like an ape? Or maybe how I fell, ass-over-head, right over the top of their chair? I don't know if they thought the monkey was funny. Maybe the both of us were damn funny? But, they just gasped for breath and laughed. They grabbed each other in a hug and laughed some more. They made for quite a silhouette on the front porch, through the doorway – Peter's mom and dad. I decided…I liked them.

CHAPTER 23
SWAZNOBI TRADERS AND TOURS

Breakfast came and went. I watched my pinky. Did it clutch the teacup proper? It didn't twitch anymore. I remained quiet as Peter and his parents talked. I behaved. We were busting out for China that early afternoon, and we gathered our stuff on the driveway. Not in the rental car yet though, even though it was parked right there. A van appeared on the long road to the house. I saw it was painted up as a taxi/shuttle as it came closer. Peter talked to his parents about our rental car. Dad would drive it back to the airport and drop it off. Mom would follow him and pick dad up to bring him home. Okay, all was fine in the rental car world, but why the change of plan?

Peter winked at me as he helped the cab driver load up our suitcases. A new game was afoot here, Sherlock. We sat in silence as we drove back to Capetown but drove right past the airport signs and on up the east coast. Soon, a harbor appeared to our right. Marine stores and heavy industrial stuff full of chipped paint and rust. We turned down some industrial streets toward ships and docks heading for huge erector sets of swinging cargo cranes, towers and construction pieces around. We headed for impossibly large warehouses and ships that looked altogether too enormous to be docked right off shore. I guess the water was quite deep.

The shuttle let us out by a ratty, metallic company building that read, 'Swaznobi Traders.' The cab was unloaded. Peter paid.

"We couldn't talk at the house or in the cab," Peter said as the cab drove away. "But we have changed our plans."

"Okay."

"I was in connection last night with New York. Lots of chatter last night. News from China, too. Your police Ape friends did guess we are bound for China. There is some talk that they want the Chinese officials to try and stop us when we land at the airport in Shanghai. Suspicion of kidnapping charges."

"Okay."

"They don't know where we are yet. Africa is a surprise stop to them. The Five Apes think that you have fully regained your mental senses, and you are righting a wrong and leading the charge to free the innocent and take revenge on the guilty."

"I am the Lone Ranger."

"They have contacted the Triads in Shanghai, too."

"The Customs and the Triads. Okay."

"If we get through Customs, then the Triads will try to stop us."

"Okay. Well. That's some bad shit then."

"But we will not be landing at the airport."

"Boat?"

"Boat."

We picked up our luggage and walked into the lobby of Swaznobi Traders. I just followed Peter. What do I know?

I'm a stranger in paradise. We went through some double doors and into a bay area. It looked and smelled like any warehouse full of warehouse stuff on a dock.

A white woman strutted up to us. She was in her late forties, stocky leaning toward overweight, with thinning long hair that was sprayed back and up in the air like Bed-Head met Mad Max, ridiculous tattoos by the way, work clothes with torn-off sleeves, a gold tooth, and she just looked like she stunk worse than the gunky water swirling around the dock posts outside.

"Dirty Paws, this is Rusty," Peter said.

The woman smiled big. More gold teeth stuck out. She put up her gnarly hand and shook mine. She did stink. Calloused hand, too.

"Donna Charms," she said. "They call me Dirty Paws. Usually."

"Dirty Paws is my old SAS friend I told you about," Peter said.

"I thought it was a 'he' and 'he' was in Shanghai?" I said, with a smile, so as not to appear to be the prick I tend to naturally be.

"Yeeah. I go between there and here a lot. Got business here. Got business there," she said. She didn't care what I said.

"Are we looking good to go?" Peter asked her.

"Yeeah. Looking good to go. Come on." She waved her hand as she turned, and we followed her to the rear of the place. Giant, back double doors were wide open, and men loaded wooden boxes on platforms outside.

"We're going on by boat," Peter said to me, pointing at a ship right on the pier. I stepped out into the sun to see it all, holding a hand over my eyes. It was a cruise ship, off-white, not one of the gigantic types you see in commercials. This was a smaller ship you might say, but one for the very rich, and it was big and looked seaworthy. A tall, black guy walked up and handed me a ball cap. He gave one to Peter too. The caps read 'Swaznobi Tours.' I secured it atop the old bean, the bill shadowing my face and thereby I saw it all so much better. Walk in one door and it's Swaznobi Traders and out the back door and it's Swaznobi Tours.

It wasn't the hat that made me see all of it all better though. It was a glance down into the boxes the fellas were sealing and loading in front of me. Then I understood. They were nailing up wooden crates filled with machine guns. AK-47s. I don't know too much about AKs. Never shot one. But I know one when I see one. It's a cheaper, classic, machine gun made by different companies all around the world based on the original, Russian design. The wooden crates were labeled with wine and vineyard names. I looked over at Peter.

"Smuggling. We are going to Shanghai on a gun boat that's painted up to be a cruise ship," Peter informed me.

"That looks like a cruise ship for the filthy rich." I said. Then, it made perfect sense. Sneak that in on the coast somewhere. No customs. No passports.

"Let's get on board," Dirty Paws said.

We grabbed our gear and started for the ship's ramp. She grabbed some of our stuff to help out.

"You have your medicine with you?" Dirty Paws asked me.

"Yeah."

I guess that whole, you know, 'I am normal' facade jig was up. She knew my diagnosis.

"Because Peter tells me that without your medicine, you are a homicidal maniac. I run a tight ship, Mr. Rusty, tight to plan, right on course and discipline. Every mate has his job. No upsets."

"No upsetting the mates and no murders aboard," I added.

"None. Not unless we see some Somali pirates up around the Cape. Then I'll be taking you off those pills and turn you loose."

We climbed aboard. The deck of the ship was plush, lush and Trump-approved. There were open areas with good-looking furniture, a small pool and a hot tub next to it. Then, a dining room, half under a roof and…

"Mr. Rusty, this way," Dirty Paws interrupted my tourist review. "Follow us."

A tall, gaunt man in a white dinner jacket and shirt with unnecessarily deep, black-dyed hair that looked like a helmet, met us at the first mahogany double doors to the inner ship.

"Jan, take these men to their rooms. See to their adjustments."

"Certainly," Jan, the Helmet Head said.

Jan took us to the rooms, and they were rich-customer-friendly. I even had a balcony. I just didn't think anything needed any "adjustments."

"Hurry upstairs and meet the arriving guests. Wine and cheese at 2 p.m.," Jan advised.

A few minutes later, Peter and I rendezvoused on the deck and leaned on the dockside rail. The boys were still busy loading up their special supplies. The only thing missing was rich, cruising tourists. Then I heard a commotion from inside the warehouse, just as a line of black limos pulled away from the front of the building that we couldn't see from where we stood from the poop deck. Is that where we were? There were happy voices, men and women. Jan started setting the big dining table under the roof. Men and women, smartly, yet casually, dressed began walking out of the warehouse and down the dock. It looked like a fashion magazine review. But, they were carrying their own bags, which didn't quite fit the high-class situation. Something else didn't fit either. There were over a dozen of them, men and women, and they were all in their mid-twenties, and looked to be incredibly fit. The women were gorgeous. Wow. All of them looked like models.

"Age limit on the cruise?" I said. "No one over 25, and must be the beautiful people?"

"Yes, a bit," Peter said.

"Beauty limit?"

"They are all paid to be here. Cover," Peter said with that hard k-sound with every c-word he used. "They come on the cruise like actors to be eye candy, to look like rich, young aristocrats. Just in case the ship is stopped by authorities, or its activity questioned. But they are really all athletes. All mixed martial artists. And most are good with a gun and a knife." Peter made a motion over his scalp with his finger, which I didn't get the meaning of. Usually, people run their finger across their throat for the "killer" pantomime. Why the scalp? He smiled. "They have done other jobs for Dirty, too."

"Dirty Paws, yes, I was going to ask you. There are females in the South African SAS?"

"No. But Dirty Paws has worked hand-in-hand with us for years. We overlook her other hobbies."

Paws-in-paws. I thought about the guns. The guns. Here was Peter, Mister, you know, Freedom. Mr. Freedom, freeing the innocent and oppressed from New York City. And he knows all about this gun smuggling?

"Where do these guns go?" I asked.

"To China. To some gangs. Some revolutionaries. Sometimes they are resold from there, like to Mexico."

"The drug cartels?"

"Probably."

I felt a little dizzy. My mouth dried up. Whew. The Mexican drug cartels?

"Does Sad know about this?"

"No."

I looked at Peter's calm profile. This stoic good guy. Maybe he wasn't such a good guy. Maybe if he were as good as he could be, he would report this? Stop this? I grabbed the brass railing with both hands. Sad just thinks we are making our way to China.

"We need to operate with connections all over the world, Rusty. Some things Sad does not need to know. One paw gets dirty, so the other paw stays clean."

I nodded, but I didn't get it. I mean, I got it, dirty paw-clean paw. But I didn't like how it fleshed out. My eyes caught a twirling motion on the brass rail. It was a reflection of the spinning ceiling fan behind us. It was like a hypnotic spiral. I bore down on it. Couldn't help myself. My jaw dropped. I shook my head and got free of its spell.

I watched as each acting cruiser came on the deck. Jan piled their luggage beside the gang plank. Swank pieces. They smiled at us. They seemed to know Peter.

One said, "It's Peter!"

"Do not mess with any of them, Rusty," he said from the side of his mouth. "They are in a different league than you," Peter advised.

"You mean, the sane league?"

"No. No, they are quite deadly."

"Oh, a...killing league," I said.

Huh? I am too cool to fully respond to that one, being a level two, street-sweeping bad ass killer myself. So what league is that exactly? Are they, not to be messed with? Level three, or above? Cause hey, killing is killing in the killing league.

CHAPTER 24
DIFFERING LEAGUES FOR DIFFERENT FOLKS

We had the wine. We ate the cheese. And had other funky little food things. I was cordial. I didn't say much, and they didn't seem to care. I spent most of my time, circling the women and just…just smelling them. Just absorbing their auras. Like a leech, but I hope I wasn't too slobbery. You know my manly-man passport hasn't been stamped by a luscious, classy woman in many a year. Just speed whores and flophouse broads and hookers. Even if they were killer elites, as Peter declared, to be in a group of them like this was just sexually ridiculous.

Dirty Paws appeared from the main cabin, and she must have changed into her secret identity. She combed her thinning mop down and wore a white shirt and white pants with various seafaring insignias for the rank of a captain. The gun loading crew also emerged in various uniforms and Swaznobi Smugglers…I mean Swaznobi Traders now became Swaznobi Tours. And we left for China! Anchors up and away! How many days would it take to get there?

How many days did Downing have left on his death row wall calendar of life?

******

The first three days of this trip went fast. Ran together, in fact. There was eating. There was sleeping. There was swimming. There was sunning. The bold and beautiful all worked out in the ship's gym. There must have been some serious screwing in those cabin rooms at night. Yeah. Had to be. I sure hope so, anyway.

On the fourth day, I walked past the gym, heard the weight stacks crash and the classic gym music inside and had an itch to go in and work out. How long had it been? I was feeling okay. Taking my Zulu pills, but the fifth day? The fifth day, I had some kind of a relapse. Ceiling fans. Yeah, fans again. In the morning, I walked into the dining room off the open deck and saw every one of them. First, they just distracted me.

Now you know you see everything all the time, and just don't notice it all. But a switch in my head shack got flipped. I zeroed in on every ceiling fan all at once. In the main dining room that opened out to the deck were six fans. Some of the cabanas on the deck had fans. But there's more. On the glass tables the spinning fans were also reflected. In the silverware – on the rounded ends of the spoons and on the flats of the knives, the little distorted, misshapen fans were spinning all in a sickening unison. The windows of the dining room reflected the fans. The brass handles, the racks of glasses, Fans! Fans! Fans! The sunglasses on faces had fans spinning on them. Spinning and spinning. I became hypnotized by all the patterns. My tongue swelled. I couldn't stop searching for more reflections! How come I couldn't stop? Searching, searching for more and more fans. My windpipe swelled. Someone said something to me. I just looked at the spinning fans in their sunglasses. I turned away and went into my cabin. The hall ceilings had fans. The doorknobs had those fans. The glass on a sea painting. I had to hide away.

Hide away. Somewhere where no one could see me like this. My room had two fans. Where would the fans end? I left my fan room for the fan hall. I went down the steps. Down and around. Away from fans! It got darker. Hotter. The engines hummed loud. I opened a metal door and walked into a room. A small porthole lit half the place with sunlight. An engine room of some kind. Pipes, machinery. Heat. No fans. Nothing spinning but some gears. But, you see, gears weren't my thing. Gears were okay. Gears were cool. It was the fans! I dropped to my knees. Sick. I lay down on the metal floor. I crawled to a corner. Couldn't be found, not by man, nor beast, nor fan. I curled up around a big pipe. I panted. It was a fit. A seizure. I opened my eyes real quick to hunt for a fan. No fans. None. I had the urge to look in a mirror, to see if there were spinning fans in my eyes. But I shut down instead. I shut down. Got small. There was a rag on the floor. It was dirty, but I bit into it. Then I fell asleep. Or I passed out? I don't know. I don't know! How long? I don't know.

Hours later? Days later? The metal door opened with a screech, and my eyes popped open. The room was dark, but the half-open vents of a porthole showed daylight outside. How long was I there? I felt like cement on the cold gray metal floor. Was someone looking for me? I looked up from my corner, expecting to see Peter, Dirty Paws, Jan or a Mr. or Miss Adonis. No! What? It was a skinny black guy, a stranger dressed in a gross tank top and tan Capri pants. And then I saw the machine gun he held hip high. His eyes made a quick scan of the room, but at a high level. I couldn't have moved if I wanted to. I was still half asleep in a brain sick coma.

The guy left. Shut the door behind him. I knew this was not right. I sat up, turned onto my knees and stood with the help of the pipes around me. What was going on here? I walked to the door. I guessed when the guy would have left the hall and opened the noisy metal door a crack. The hall was clear. I didn't know much, but I knew I had to get to my pistol in my bags in my room. These truths I hold to be self-evident. I went down the hall, slipped up the stairs, then down that hall to my room. My door was left open? Lock and handle broken. There had been a search there, too. I stepped in and shut the door behind me. My bags were not searched though. I opened the big one, pulled a Glock that Peter gave me from inside a folded towel, and I found two magazines loose at the bottom. I slid one in. Stuck the other magazine in my pocket.

Out I went. Down the hall. Down the next hall to the Captain's bridge. This place would overlook the whole front of the ship. A machine gun blast! Some cheering in the distance! Foreign cheering and in a foreign language! It made me duck. What the...? But I instinctively knew what was happening. Yeah. A hijack. This was a hijack, and I spazzed right through it.

I got to the door of the bridge upstairs, and it was half glass. Another burst of gunfire outside! I started to peer into the bridge a few inches at a time. An inch. An inch. There's Captain Dirty Paws, her back to me. There's one of the crew – the first mate. They are looking at something. An inch more. An inch more. A tall, thin black male in ragged shorts and a shirt. He was sneering. He was talking to Dirty Paws with a lecture tinged voice and face. He had a rifle in his hand, the barrel aimed downward. Outside, off in the distance came another louder barrage of machine gun fire. And yelling. Lots of yelling. Cheering. Inch more.

Inch more. Saw another thin black male who had his back to the door, looking out the front window. A machine gun, probably his, lay across the control board in front of him.

Matey, thar be pirates! Freakin' African pirates. I could already tell I didn't like pirates. With no great haste, I calmly opened the door and the pirate facing Dirty Paws just as casually looked up at me. I guess because I opened the door slowly his eyes just glanced up and he continued talking. I shot that bastard right in the throat. Then I shot that other bastard square in the back once and once in the back of the head, all before the first guy hit the floor, gurgling. Both in about two seconds.

Dirty Paws jumped aside and, with the widest of eyes, looked me over. Then we looked out the windows. Four more pirates held all our magnificent cruise guests at bay, all sitting, ass on the deck in lines. Even Peter was trapped among them, all in bathing suits. Most of the crew were also in attendance too, in their uniforms under the pirate guns. The pirates thought nothing of my gunshots, since they were erupting all over.

"There!" Dirty Paws pointed to a mid-sized boat not far away. I could see additional pirates with guns manning the deck. "They snuck up on us in a raft from that boat. And that is not the mothership. I don't know where the mothership is. They always have one."

I saw the boat. Held about 10 guys. All with long guns, and one had a rocket propelled grenade. They were dressed in various military uniforms or civilian clothes. There were long, torn streamers like flags on posts on the sides. They wore hats, or those stocking skull cap things black people wear for their hair. They looked like a scene from Costner's "Water World" movie to me. Sci-fi.

The first mate began unlocking some cabinets and pulled out two AK-47s.

"Prime the dual 50 cals," Dirty told the first mate, while checking the rifle she was handed.

"Want one?" she asked me.

"No. I'll stick with this." I raised my pistol.

Hell, I never shot a machine gun before. I'll stick with what I know. I changed mags in what I know.

Dirty got herself a 9mm pistol too from the cabinet. The first mate opened the wall. What I first thought was just a back wall, was actually a hidden door. He charged up a narrow hallway of stairs behind it. Dirty and I left the bridge, and we started down a side stairway.

"Watch out behind…" Dirty Paws started to tell me, but then she saw I was already watching out behind us. "I'll start out shooting to the left. You the right," she whispered.

We walked out the front deck. Four pirates stood there facing the hostages. As planned, Dirty Paws did her thing. She belted the pirate to her left with a burst of AK. The guy's body riddled with the shock waves. Passengers and crew dropped to the deck like pros. Not a sound amongst them. I shot the guy on the far right about 3 times, as Dirty Paws hit her next jerk as he barely started to turn on us. The final pirate did turn, and we both shot him down. The crew and "guests" scrambled on all fours for the fallen guns.

Dirty Paw shouted above, "Go hot!"

I looked up over the bridge in time to see two sections atop the bridge fall open on hinges, and the first mate stood behind two big military, machine guns mounted on one single podium.

"Going hoooooot!" he cried out and opened fire out toward the ocean. I could feel the gunfire shake my lungs. I ran to the side. These rounds sliced into the water in front of the pirate's boat. Then the rounds walked up into the boat itself. The massive fire power pelted through the boat and the people on it. The bullets ripped and tore through wood, metal and bodies in a mist of swirling splinters and meat in a flurry of disintegration. The rounds smashed into the water behind the boat, creating a backdrop of white foam splashes. It was sick. It was beautiful. Magic revenge.

A woman in a bikini leaned over the side with a dead pirate's machine gun in her hands and opened fire. I ran nearby to see that, too. Peter, in his disgusting little red Speedo, joined her. They shot up the raft below and two guys inside it.

The men yelled, "no...noooo!"

Peter yelled, "yes...yeeees!"

Then the aftermath. The relief. Dirty Paws began tossing out orders.

"Get us out of here!" she shouted to the machine gunner upstairs. "Full speed."

The man dropped back down into the bridge.

"Get armed and search the vessel," she told others. Some took off. "Jackson, you relieve the machine gun post."

"Aye-Aye."

I started to help the few in the search, but Dirty Paws put one of her dirty paws on my shoulder.

"Not you, my friend. My rescuer. HA! You rest here." She turned to the others. "Our friend Rusty saved the day. Killed the commanders on the bridge while they explained to me what my surrender terms would be. He came in with his pistol and shot them cold. Cold, I tell you!" She looked back at me and nodded her head. "Cold. No talking. No offers of peace. No hesitation."

"I took a bullet once in my impulse control," I tapped my head.

"HEY! Hey!" someone shouted. They all raised their weapons in my general direction! What? I turned to see the man who had searched the machine room and startled me awake. He held an AK-47 way over his head.

"I surrender! I surrender to you!" he shouted. He tossed the weapon overboard, much to the groans of dismay from some of the crew, who wanted the extra gun.

"I am under your arrest! I am under your arrest! I surrender," he said. "I wish to speak to an attorney in New York City."

What? Attorney? New York City? This instantly pissed me off. I recalled news stories on TV of other captured African pirates making this same silly request. Like they would be taken to the UN in New York or something? Must be in their pirate handbook.

"As a former representative of New York law enforcement," I said, "your request is denied." I shot that joker right in his smart-ass face. Right in the mouth. He dropped like a ton of bricks. Well, I mean he was a skinny little fucker, not heavy like a ton of… well…you know what I mean. Switch off!

I turned and everyone was looking at me.

"Eh, aha…pirates. Whew!" I said.

The ship suddenly roared to life under us, breaking their scrutiny. We all stutter-stepped with the force of it lurching forward. I didn't imagine the ship could go that fast, so quickly. This was faster than we had gone before.

Dirty Paws saw my surprise. "He has an amazing engine. Fast enough to outrun the devil himself." So a male captain calls the ship "she?" And, a female captain calls the ship "he?"

Jan, the head butler, walked up and handed me a cold bottle of water, which I took. I drank.

"He's yours," one of the guests said and handed me a huge knife.

"He's got more than one! Two more on the deck and two in the bridge," Dirty Paws said. She was bending over one of the men she shot. Doing something I couldn't see.

"Mine?" I asked.

Then I saw what Captain Dirty Paws was doing. She was scalping the pirate. Yes, I do mean scalping the head hair and head skin off the pirate's skull.

Peter came to explain. "We scalp the pirates," he said matter-of-factly. "We keep them. We can sell them if we wish to some African governments." Then I remembered Peter's little finger movement across the scalp back on the first day of this glorious cruise.

"Oh, well, yeah," I handed my knife to Peter. "Since you and Lizzie Borden over there shot those two down in the boat and can't get any souvenirs? You can have mine, too."

Peter took the knife and started in on the fallen. Lizzie followed suit.

The others looked at me.

"Scalps! Free scalps on me for everyone!" I said loudly. I didn't know what else to say.

Jan passed out bottled water to everyone and then opened some red wine. A butler connected a hose and started washing some of the blood off the deck. Dirty Paws dragged her dead guy over to the side and heaved him off the boat. She had a fist full of head hair and raised it in the air, shaking it with gleeful, deep chuckles and a huge, savage grin. Some cheered and clapped.

Three of the women scalped the rest of the dead. They looked a little different now than at breakfast when they first arrived in their little sun dresses and sandals. A little different. They were sloppy, wet, their hair a mess. Their expensive thongs and bras were covered in blood, as they scalped corpses. You know, I once sat in a stinking sewer in Bayonne, New Jersey smoking crack with three homeless bums and a runaway kid. And that seemed to make more sense to me than all of this did now.

Finished scalping, Peter tossed his guy over the side. Or rather my guy that I gave over to Peter – you know – to keep all the scalping books straight in Heaven. He stood beside me, and we watched the other hair removers in action.

"You know Peter, you were right the other day."

"Hmmm?"

"This league thing. I may shoot the occasional person. But I am not in their league."

CHAPTER 25
THE RISE OF A RED DAWN

It was dawn. A red dawn. Several days had come and gone, and now the ship crept into a small Chinese harbor. I could tell by the dawn lights on the coast it was a small city, or a village even? I stood near the bow, in the wet chill, with a cup of South African coffee in hand, ready to get this nasty day under way. The collar of my big, black leather trench coat was up. My Swaznobi Tours ball cap pulled tight on my head. We were south of Shanghai, dodging the main port's customs and inspectors. We hoped anyway. The full crew was awake, up, their gaze searching the horizon now like me.

Peter joined me with his own cup of coffee. I nodded. We scanned. We did see some small fishing boats hitting the waterways.

"Dirty Paws will have a car waiting for us," he said.

"Good. How long a drive?"

"About three hours into the city. We don't have to go deep into the city."

"Okay."

"She is coming with us."

"She is?"

"She is and another man, too. A good man named Jonas. She says she owes us. You for what you've done. Me, for all the other missions we've done together. She'd be dead years ago if not for me. And now she owes you, too."

"Okay."

"She knows the city. Good and bad. We get our man and get him back here. We'll leave by boat. Tonight. While we're gone, the crew will unload their gun shipment. Disperse it to the customers. Dirty was going to stay here for a while anyway, but now she will help us get our man back out."

"You know we're probably going to have to get his son, too," I warned. "I bet he won't leave without his son."

"Christ!" Peter cursed with that heavy 'k'. "You're probably right."

"Best be ready for that."

"Yeah. You have your passport?"

"Yeah."

"You have your guns?"

"Yeah. Two of them. Lots of ammo."

"Vest?"

"On."

"You got your Chinese money?"

"Got my Chinese money."

"Take your pill?"

"Pill taken."

"How are you feeling?"

"I don't know, Peter. The usual. Every day's an out-of-body experience."

Peter nodded. We quietly, slowly cut through the water.

"China," I muttered. "You been?"

"Yes, I have been…on…business. With Dirty."

******

We approached a dock. People stood there. One of them waved a lantern. There were three small trucks with crazy, foreign writing on them. China smelled different. Maybe it was the smell of their breakfast food in the air? Maybe this was just what China smelled like?

Dirty Paws crossed the deck to the dock side of our ship. She waved. She spoke Chinese. They spoke to her. There were some smiles. Some not. Four of our guys stood near Dirty Paws, holding machine guns just below the side wall, out of the dock's line of sight below. Some security measures. They had guys standing around. They were no doubt packing, too. Their security.

Other men busied themselves below pulling the ship into position. There was work to be done. Gun smuggling work. Then our gig. I took a big swig of my cooling coffee. So Dirty Paws was coming with us. Good. She's like three Green Berets and a roller derby team rolled into one. I felt much better with her on the team. Team? Listen to me talk all kinds of Army smack.

******

I sat in the back of the big sedan. A foreign name car I could not even read. Jonas got behind the wheel. Dirty sat up front. Peter got in the back with me.

"Good morning," Dirty Paws said.

"Good morning," I replied.

Someone put a big duffle bag in the trunk, shut it and then rapped on it twice. Jonas started the car, and we drove off, up through the village, to a main road and then followed that one along to a pretty modern looking highway.

Dirty Paws spoke up.

"Let's all get on the same page," she said. "We are

getting a guy who works in a medical clinic."

"Bo Zoup," I said.

"He was a Chinese diplomat in New York City. This guy's wife was murdered because he would not cooperate with smugglers. The smugglers were corrupt cops and a Chinese Triad."

"And the New York Mob," I said.

"They all needed him to press through a trade agreement which concealed the smuggling of drugs. Heroin."

She turned in her seat and rested part of her back on the door, and she looked right at us and continued, "The corrupt cops set up an innocent man for the murder. A patsy. But the diplomat knew all along the murderers where these cops."

"And the Mob," I added again.

"And the mobsters," she repeated.

"Heroin. China sends. Cops receive. Mob sells."

"You got it."

"The diplomat pushed the trade treaty through after the murder. China finds out. Involved or not, Zoup is disgraced. They put him to work in a plastic surgery clinic. Years later, you have found out about the innocent patsy. You are trying to clear this patsy. Save him before his execution. You need the diplomat to testify."

I nodded.

"What makes you think he will testify?"

"He has to testify now," I said. "They will kill him either way. They will use him to draw us in and stop us. Then kill him as a loose end."

"He has to cooperate with us," Peter said.

We hit a big bump, and Dirty slugged Jonas in the arm for it.

"What are we facing?" Peter asked.

"We are facing a Triad. The Shenyang. I know them. I know some of them. I've done protection work for one of their daughters during a Triad war. The families were threatened, and all the family members body-guarded up. Nice kid. But, they have a lot of young bulls dripping testosterone. Lots of guns. I figure the worst. I figure they don't know we are here yet, but I figure they are watching the diplomat and, when we white boys and girls show up, calls will be made and bulls and their big guns will come a running."

Peter and I exchanged glances.

"These boys will shoot up the streets anytime, any-where they want to. 9 mils. Semi-auto pistols and full-auto machine pistols. This.." she hit the interior roof with her knuckles, "is a protection car. It is bullet proof. We get your man in this car, and we can tank our way out."

"We will probably have to get his son. He won't leave without his son."

Dirty seemed nonplussed with that.

"He is a school kid. Is school in session here now? This time of year?" I asked.

She looked at Jonas.

"Yes. It is," Jonas said.

"We will have to find out where the school is from Zoup and go get the kid," I said.

"We'll get the kid. We have GPS. We can do that," she said.

I looked out the window at the very strange landscape and businesses and houses along the Chinese Highway. I worried that we'd get Bo and then be followed or chased to the school and there could be a machine gun shootout at a school. Good God!

"I'll get some aerial maps of the clinic," she said, work-ing the GPS map device on the dashboard.

It was quiet while Dirty worked. She got a satellite photo of the medical building on the screen.

"Back alley. Up the alley. Got to be a back door. We'll get in there."

We nodded.

"Anything happen? We get split up? Get to an airport and fly out," Dirty advised. "Forget the South African Embassy or the American Embassy. Fly out. Do not fly to Taiwan. The Shenyang is also there. Fly to Cairo. Fly to Dubai. Fly to Stockholm. Grab the next possible flight to a place you think Chinese Triads are not. Guess. You have money? Cards?"

"Yes," Peter said.

"Don't go back to the ship. If something really bad happens and we split up, I am ordering the ship to leave."

"If we fly our man out, he'll need a passport," I said.

"Yes, he will," Peter said. "They will be back at his house. Father and son."

"Shit," Dirty said. "Well…we'll see. We'll see what happens."

It got quiet. I stared out the window. We hit the outskirts of Shanghai. It looked like any other city that took a bath in Chinatown. Well, bath is a bad word, it was filthy in parts. It got more dense the deeper we got. More Chinese-looking. More small people. More small cars. Small buildings. Small. Smaller. I got that tightness in my throat. I closed my eyes. Not now. Not now. Not now. No. I tried to breathe deep, but not let it be obvious that I was struggling to hang on to my sanity. I leaned back against the head rest, pretending to go to sleep. I stayed in this limbo. I kept one finger on the limbo ledge, hanging there like a parrot in a cage with a claw outside the cage, just to feel the wind of the outside world on my claw. Like…

…the car stopped. We were there. The dash clock read 10 a.m. All four of us popped our doors and stepped outside. We were parked in an alley, an alley off of another alley that could have been anywhere in the world. Trash cans. Dumpsters. Junk. Soil. Dirt. Stink. Cars going by at the end of the alley.

"Jonas," Dirty Paws said. "You wait here."

The three of us walked up the alley. The medical building had a set of glass doors for the alley. Unlocked. We walked right in. We turned for the street side lobby and the décor improved the closer we got to it.

Dirty looked at a giant sign on the wall. She read the Chinese.

"Third floor, Suite 3-12. Where are the stairs?"

We looked around and saw the stairs.

"Just want to know where they are," Dirty said.

We got on the elevator. She hit the button with the abstract art scratch that must be "3" in Chinese. The doors opened. Peter and I followed Dirty down the hall. We walked into a suite. It wasn't plush, but it wasn't a plumber's office either. Several girls, you know, teens and some in their 20s were seated there, all engaged in telephone conversations or reading stuff on their cell phones. None looked suspicious. All girls looking to convert their eastern eyes to western eyes. They barely noticed us.

Dirty walked to the counter where three women in white smocks worked away on whatever paperwork they do to turn eastern eyes to western eyes.

Dirty spoke.

Woman at counter spoke. Counter woman looked unhappy. Non-compliant.

Dirty spoke again. I heard Zoup's name in the mix.

Other woman in white chimed in. Looked unhappy. Non-compliant.

Dirty acted non-compliant.

The third woman in white conferred with the other two. Then she walked off into the back. Dirty wandered over to us.

"What did you say?" Peter asked.

"I told them that I wanted eyelid surgery. I wanted eastern eyes. They told me they did not do that. They only made western eyes. I told them I wanted eastern eyes, and wanted to speak to the manager, one that I had talked to about this on the phone. A Mr. Zoup."

The lobby door opened, and we were led into the back, down a hall and in front of a closed door. The woman said something to Dirty. Dirty replied. She opened the door. I could see a bland, but big-sized room. Zoup was behind a desk in a suit and tie. He looked up with wide eyes, and he looked nervous times ten.

Dirty walked in. Peter walked in next. Me next. But, Peter took off to the right like a receiver for the New York Giants. Another step in, and I saw why. In the right corner was a little thug with a Mohawk Hairdo and a tattoo on his face, in a black leather pant suit, seated in a chair. Peter had drawn his pistol and held it point blank at this little punk. I shut the door.

Dirty growled something at said punk. I got the translation. It was something like "go ahead, move and die, fuck-nuts." Something like that.

I looked at Mister Zoup. He looked at me.

"Hands," I said, waving my right hand upward. He knew to put his hands on the desk.

"You remember me?" I asked.

"Yes."

"You are a dead man," I told him, ready to start my speech on how he should come with us and testify.

"We are all dead," Zoup said. "They knew you were coming."

The door burst open behind me. But the sound was more than just a door hitting the wall. A machine gun? I ducked off to the left, and Dirty dropped to the floor, pulling her gun. Peter flattened out against the wall. Zoup dropped behind his desk as the rounds flew over his head into the wall and windows behind him. Zoup was target one. He'd lured the hunting party into the trap.

One of those desk women in the white smocks held a machine pistol in the doorway, and she screamed like a banshee, blasting away. Dirty shot from the floor, stitching up the woman's body until she dropped the gun and fell back into the hall. She was a perforated mess. And the red stains were growing fast on the white outfit. There were many screams from the lobby. There is no place more like hell than being in a small room with a machine pistol going off.

Peter killed the guy in the corner, flat out. I mean, why have him hang around now? Peter pilfered the punk's pistol and two mags. I got around the desk, and Zoup was huddled down and still unventilated. I got him up. Peter and Dirty were already clearing the hallway.

"Your son?"

"He lives with his grandmother now. But they will use him to keep me quiet. To keep me here. To make me surrender to them."

"Where is he now?"

"At his school."

"Take us there."

I grabbed his arm and pulled him over the dead woman. I picked up her machine pistol. I pulled the magazine to see some rounds left inside. Then shoved it back into place. I walked him to the end of the hallway where Peter and Dirty waited.

"Who else?" Peter asked, as we got closer.

"The man in the room, and the girl. They were the only ones watching me," Zoup said.

"Any idea of backup in the street? Across the street? Any cars? Anybody?"

"I don't know."

"Let's go."

We stepped through the abandoned lobby and out of the suite. We jogged down the hall. Dirty hit the elevator button. A ruse for any elevator watchers, because we went right past it to the stairs.

"Let me have that," Peter ordered when we arrived at the stairwell. He knew I was new to machine guns. I handed him the weapon, and he handed me the thug's pistol and mags. No problem. I will let the adults play with the machine guns. Especially if the adults were SAS combat vets.

"Magazine about half full," I told him. "Round in chamber."

He nodded.

"Ready?" Peter said.

"Ready," Dirty said.

Peter pointed to my face and then pointed up the stairs. I can take a hint. I am the one looking upstairs while we walk downstairs.

We started down the steps. Fast, but careful. We all knew that crazy woman had time to call the local crime boss and tell them my special business party had arrived early. We had a few minutes. Maybe. Down the stars, down the stairs.

Dirty dialed her cell phone. "Back it up to the doors," Dirty whispered, obviously to Jonas waiting outside.

Down more stairs. First floor. To the back. To the alley doors. Peter stepped out quickly, his machine pistol ready. He swept the barrel right and left. Left and right. Then up. The black sedan finished backing up. Dirty opened the side doors. Me, first in the back. Then Soup. Dirty got into the front. Peter was last in the back seat.

Jonas hit the gas pretty hard, but no tires screeched. I don't know if you could make this heavy tank screech tires. So far so good. THEN…

…one of these chink hoods appeared at the corner of the alley. He held a bigger machine gun than his buddy had. And he opened up on our car with it. Man, I mean full bore. We all reflexively ducked. These rounds pelted the car, and Jonas kept driving right up to him. No other way out now. I realized that none of the bullets penetrated the "protection" car. The glass merely buckled in. Small circle patterns and the sound? Sounded like…well, like bullets hitting heavy metal, but I felt each one in my clavicle notch with a dry gulp. It was especially bad when we drove past the guy. He was close. He looked like a guy in a science fiction movie. Hair spiked up. Weird clothes. Weird jewelry. He showed a lot of teeth as he blasted us from the hip. We blasted by him and the right-side windows took a beating. A lot of rounds hit us, and they showed it in cracked patterns. I couldn't believe the doors and windows held. I didn't know what to think. We would all be dead if not for this special car. Jonas turned the corner onto the street and off we went.

"Everyone okay?" Dirty asked.

I coughed. Peter pushed his finger on the glass next to him to check it out. Jonas made a hard right and slung us all over a bit in our seats. Dirty Paws did not slug him in the arm this time.

"The school," I reminded Zoup.

"Turn left."

Dirty and Peter reloaded. The machine pistol must have been a nine. Peter filled it with his own pistol bullets.

"Turn here. Left here. They will know where I am going," Zoup said, his hands quivering on the top of the seat in front of us.

"You knew that Steverino Downing didn't kill your wife. That these punks did," I had to say it. I stared at his profile. "Why didn't you say anything?"

"Turn right. Go straight for about five minutes." His English was impeccable. "You know the answer, Detective. They would kill me, too. Kill my son. All I could do was to sit quiet and let the trial proceed. Then prepare the trade treaty, which passed even before the murder trial was finished."

"Ever think of telling me? Passing the news to me? Secretly?"

"You? You! You ever hear of the Five Apes, Detective? For all I knew, you were in the Five Apes. How could I trust you? How could I trust anyone? My government transferred me back home because of the crime. The shame of it. But somehow, they knew the truth about the treaty and the murder of my wife. Somehow." He turned and looked at me. "They have people like the Five Apes here in China too, Detective."

"I am not a detective anymore."

"Then why are doing all this?" Zoup said with anger, and he pounded the seat top. "This was over! It was over for my son and me!"

I had an answer for him all pent up inside me, a damn good answer in my mind. Like a speech. But it wouldn't leave my mouth. Instead, I said, "Yeah, well, it will be over for Downing in about two weeks. It's not over for him yet."

"We are all going to die now. Instead of just Downing. He will die anyway, and now we all will die." Zoup said aloud to no one in particular. A public service announcement.

And no one looked at me, but I knew what they were thinking. Zoup could be right.

CHAPTER 26
OUT-CRAZED

The school was down a long, hilly street, with some trees breaking out of the solid city concrete. We saw no suspicious cars or people. Some kids played out front of the building, hanging off of, and swinging on, a colorful cartoon-like contraption I could not recognize on the playground. Some teachers stood around them, half-watching, half-talking. We pulled up to the front and parked.

"Let me and Zoup walk in. Why don't you guys troll the lot out here," I said.

They nodded, and we all got out of the car. Dirty went to the trunk and opened it. I looked in. She zipped open a big canvas black bag, and I saw several AK-47s. She looked them over, closed down the truck lid but not all the way until it clicked, for quick access.

Zoup and I crossed the short front lawn by the kids to a set of double doors. This got us right into the school office. And inside? You could have cut this office air with a knife. Every woman working in the large room behind the long wooden counter cut their eyes to us. Grim, thin-lipped expressions. And there were two men in there. Both standing. Both in dress clothes. One on one side and one on the other. 30s. Short, greased back black hair. And not sci-fi looking guys like we just saw at the clinic. They just stood there with tough guy grimaces.

Zoup walked across the lobby, and I stopped and turned back to the door to look at Peter, Jonas and Dirty. I stepped a bit off to a point where I though the doomsday duo inside wouldn't see me, and mouthed the word, "Trap."

I think they got it. Trouble in Chinatown. Big trouble.

I walked in behind Zoup. I had both my hands in my pockets and a pistol in each hand. Safeties off. Rounds in chambers.

Zoup said something to a woman behind the counter. She was a terrible actress if she was trying to look normal. She looked at the man to her left and walked out a back door. Hells bells, this was not good. The two guys were packing under those suit coats, too. How's about a shootout in a school of cute, innocent, little Chinese kids? And shit! These poor workers and teachers?

I stared at the guy to the left. A stare down contest.

"Zoup," I said. I let go of a gun, pulled out my hand and used a finger for him to follow me. I walked around the corner of the counter and re-grabbed the hidden pistol in my pocket again. Zoup followed. And I walked right up to this guy. He half sneered.

"Tell him, we don't have to do this. Tell him we don't want any trouble."

Zoup translated.

"Tell him, my friends and I will leave, and leave you and the boy here. We do not want to have a shootout in a school."

Zoup looked confused. Like I was suddenly leaving him to the dogs of war.

The other guy walked up to us. This was good. Before I started killing people, I wanted to absolutely confirm they were Triad.

"Tell him!" I ordered Zoup.

Zoup told him. The two men looked at each other, then one said something to Zoup.

"They said they would have to call their boss."

Triad confirmed. And, I shot both those fuckers. The one on the right with my right gun, the one on my left from my left gun. My coat pockets erupted open. Put rounds in their chests. I knew that since the guns were fired inside my pockets, they might both be disabled because the shells couldn't eject! I let go of the left one, and I pulled my right gun out of the burned pocket and racked the slide. Sure enough the shell had stove-piped in the ejection port. I racked the slide and cleared the shell, and I shot like hell. I shot and shot both guys. They stumbled back and fell in a chaotic, wild, arms-swinging messes. This pistol ran empty, and I pulled the other out and racked that slide. The office was in pandemonium. Pandemonium – I always liked that word.

"Any more?" I yelled to Zoup.

He asked the women. Some answered. Most scattered.

"In the back office," Soup said. He pointed to a door on the back wall.

"Get their guns and their ammo," I told Zoup.

He crawled over to the bodies, still writhing a bit.

"Where's your kid?" I whispered in desperation. "Tell them we need your kid, and we will leave."

Crouched, gun up, I made for the back-office door. It must have been a principal's room of some kind. I got close. I heard a guy yelling. I sliced the pie of the open door and saw an old Chinese guy sitting in a corner looking 10 shades of scared to hell. He wasn't the one talking. Must have been the civilian office holder. Another was. I sliced my view further and saw my third bad guy. He was holding a pistol in one hand and yelling into a phone. He was mad looking because his little stake-out job went to shit. He probably thought he'd be dealing with reasonable, law-abiding people. He probably thought he had the upper hand, that they were the only crazy ones. Guess again, numb-nuts, cause you have been out-crazed.

He saw me peek in. I saw him raise his pistol, and I jumped back. He didn't shoot. A woman ran into the front officer behind me. There was a boy with her. Zoup clutched him. We got the kid! I heard machine gun fire coming from the parking lot! The guy in the back office called out the Triad cavalry. I ran to a big wooden desk and shoved it in front of the back-office door. Then I shoved another one next to it. Yeah, the door was open, but our man in the office would have to at least crawl across the tops of these desks to get out, slowing him down. He couldn't just dash out. But he could still shoot from there!

By now, the employees left the office, doing whatever school employees do when a gunfight blows up in the front office. There was just me, Zoup and his son, kneeling by the doors. I kept an eye on the back-office door in case boss man tried to escape. He peeked out once, and I shot at him. Missed. But he got the message. Peeky-a-boo and get shot.

The machine gun fire increased out front, and I peered out over a windowsill. There were two tones to the gunfire. Our side, and their side. On the left, Dirty, Jonas and Peter were behind our tank car, taking turns shooting over to the right. And on the right set a black sedan. Inside sat two thugs holding machine pistols inside. Their car was not a tank and was eating the live AK rounds. Windows gone and vehicle heavily perforated.

Across the hall I saw a set of doors and long hallway with more doors. If I could get down there, I could flank these two jerks on the lot and shoot them, almost from behind.

"Get me those guns."

Zoup handed me the two pistols and several magazines. I looked at one. Round in chamber and safety off. I gave it back to him.

"You use this. We are going down that hall. That guy in the office may follow us, and you have to shoot him if he does. I am not going to ask you if you can do that. You have no choice. You shoot him, or we die."

We all ran across the hall and got into that other hallway. Kids and adults were screaming and running out the far end. Then we piled into the first classroom on the left, already abandoned, and I ran to the windows. I couldn't see the bad guys out these windows! Damn cartoon statues and playground stuff. I opened the window and, headfirst, slipped out onto the gravel of the playground. I got a pistol ready in each hand, stood, sucked in a deep breath, and I ran for the sedan, across the candy cane obstacle course of smiling, weird ducks, mice and…whatever those Chinese things were.

The sides of the bad guys came into full view and, with both guns, I shot at them and charged. I might have screamed. I might have yelled. My bullets pelted them like fast-pitch baseballs in the legs, in the arms and in their heads. They collapsed down in a heap, and I shot until I stood right over them. Peter knew when to charge, too. And he ran right up to the other end of the car, AK at the ready.

In the new stillness, I heard sirens. We needed to leave. I reloaded while I ran to the front doors. Peter followed.

"I got one loose in here."

We burst in. Peter watched the hall and main office. I cut back down the school hallway. I turned into that first classroom. A dead guy lay in the doorway, face down. I didn't know who…but on the far wall sitting on the floor under the window, Zoup sat. His left arm around his son. His right hand held that pistol I gave him resting it on his thigh. Do or die, I told him. Zoup do. Zoup shot that bossman.

"We got to go!" My arm waved for them.

They got up, stepped over the dead guy, and we all four left the building.

"Rusty has left the building," I said aloud to myself. "Thank you very much."

CHAPTER 27
ESCAPE FROM SHANGHAI

We jumped into the car. Jonas hit the gas pedal, and we drove down the hill, rather than hit the main avenue at the top. The GPS guided us away from the blood bath. Everyone was stone cold silent. I got a good look at the kid, now about 13 years old, and I could tell he was in shock. His jaw just hung low.

"You did good Zoup. You saved us. You saved us all, and nobody died," I said.

"They died."

"Yeah, they died, but they were the bad guys. They don't count. No good people died."

Zoup just stared ahead.

"And now, Downing won't die either."

Zoup looked at his son. "Those were the men that killed your mother," he said.

The kid looked confused and shocked. Then they spoke in Chinese. It was slow. It was emotional. I could guess what was said. A few tears fell down across Zoup's mouth.

The horror story unfolded. The whole story. The true story.

"We are not out of this yet," Dirty Paws said. "We have to get this hunk of shot up junk back to the harbor. And every cop in Shanghai may be looking for it now."

She was right. Bullet proof or not, it was a pulverized wreck and a walking advertisement for trouble. What if the Shenyang Triad was searching the streets for us?

"Let's rent a car. Can we rent a car? We'll ditch this, and all we need is three or four hours to get back to the harbor," I suggested.

"Who'll rent it?" Dirty asked.

"I can," Zoup said.

"No, better not be you. They may learn you are at the center of all this and tag your credit card for activity," I said.

"I'll rent a car," Peter said. "Rest assured, I will not be returning to China again, and so what if they connect me."

"You have false ID anyway!" I reminded him.

"Of course!"

"I will type in a rental car place on the way," Dirty said, reaching for the GPS panel.

She found one. We drove another 45 minutes and parked up the street from a rental car facility. Zoup and Peter got out and walked onto the lot. Zoup would translate. Fifteen minutes later, with Zoup behind the wheel, they left the lot in a suburban-shaped vehicle, and we followed them. Jonas turned down some side streets from the main avenue. Peter must have told him to pull over by a public park. We did the same. It was a park by a river, and there were even people doing Tai Chi out there. We got out of our decimated wreck. Peter got the big black bag from the trunk, and we all boarded the suburban.

I don't know about these other people, but I was exhausted. About an hour later, Dirty told Jonas to pull over by a market. She got out and came back with a small cardboard box of fruit, cookies and some water bottles. I ate something that looked like a green apple. Tasted like a bad mango, but hell if I cared. Drank water. Then we took off.

It was sunset when we drove back down through the winding roads of the fishing village. Dirty had been talking to her crew by phone. It sounded like we were ready to leave as soon as we stepped aboard.

"You are going to take a fantastic cruise now," I said to the son. "We are going to South Africa, then fly to the United States. We have friends there, and you will live there safely."

Zoup smiled, small and ironically. "He has always wanted to live back in the states. He wants to be an engineer. He wants to live in Silicon Valley. If he can get a Visa."

"We'll do better than a Visa," I said. Peter smiled.

We parked on the dock. I walked away from the suburban and slowly climbed the bridge to the ship. It was like home. Home base. It felt like home. Each step was like a breath of fresh air. Once aboard, I just stood there watching everyone else come up and on board. I watched the kid's face as he walked on and looked around. Even Zoup looked a little astonished. Some of the "crew" and the beautiful people came out and met them. One waved and nodded at me. I nodded back. Peter told a few of them in brief sentences what had happened. Their jaws dropped. They oohed and ahhhed. Oh yeah.

Dirty was still down on the dock talking to some Chinese people. These people got into the suburban and drove off. It would be smart to return it to the company and let the transaction just disappear in the files as perfectly normal. She and the first mate walked down the dock looking over the boat.

I walked to the front, took off my jacket and sat on a deck chair.

"Nice work, Rusty," someone said as they passed by.

Jan walked up and took my jacket. He looked over the blown-out pockets.

"Non-repairable, sir."

"Like my senses."

I could feel the ship's engine rev up. I don't know how but even that feel, that hum relaxed me more.

"A late dinner will be served after we get out to sea a bit."

"Ten-four on that. Listen, Jan, you got a movie camera on this ship?"

"Yes, we do."

"Do you have a way to film something and then upload it to the internet? To send it... anywhere?"

He pointed to the giant antenna system on the top of the bridge, next to where the secret machine gun was concealed. I nodded.

"After dinner, I need to film our new guest. I need to interview him and then send it to New York."

"We can do that. Our commo man can do that. We often send footage around the globe."

"Okay. Hey, just throw that jacket away."

"We have a Swaznobi Cruise jacket you may have sir, should you get chilly."

"And I'll be proud to wear it."

******

After dinner, Jan led Peter, Zoup and me into a room off of the bridge with a big table. One of the men had set up a tripod with a small movie camera atop it. He was waiting for us. I sat Zoup down in front of the camera, with me in a seat to the side. Peter also sat. Peter worked for Sad's firm, and was licensed, and I thought it a good idea for him to be present in the film.

"Probably...you don't need to be here. I have to name

everyone on the film, and we don't want you to be on the record. It's a legal thing," I said to the crewman.

He nodded.

"Zoup, we will not discuss anything that happened today. Just answer my questions about why your wife was murdered and what happened years ago."

"Oh hey, can you flip that so we can see what's on the film?"

The guy flipped the little camera screen over, and we saw ourselves in the viewfinder screen. I positioned myself and Zoup to better spots.

"Just turn that on." The guy did and left. I identified myself, Peter and then I asked for Zoup's full name and birthday. I asked Zoup what he did in New York and then what really happened to his wife. I'd done this kind of thing a few thousand times as a detective. It felt good. It felt natural. I had my old voice again. But it wasn't good for ol' Zoup. Not good at all. This took him back into the details. How they pressured him. How they threatened him. The night when his wife disappeared. The next day when she was found. He had nothing left in him after our bloody rescue. No protection for his soul. No barriers. He cried. He lost it. He lost it at that point. This has happened in my interviews before. I myself as an interviewer show no empathy unless empathy is needed to get the suspect or witness to continue. It was a long day for Zoup. He'd killed a man. He'd rescued his son. He evacuated. He escaped. He fled. And now he confessed to this conspiracy of threats, murder and smuggling heroin, a pawn for everyone. Even me.

Peter got him some water. On film.

"I did not tell anyone because these men would kill me. They would kill my son."

"Thank you, and this concludes our interview."

We were done. I stood and found the red button on the camera that turned it off.

Zoup ran his hands through his hair. Then he shook his head.

"You're a man in a mess, not of your own making," Peter said. "You are a victim."

"My wife was the victim. My son."

"You too, Zoup," I added.

I stepped outside the room and found our commo man out on the deck.

"Hey, man! I need to send this to New York City."

I took a deep breath of sea air. With every inch we moved forward on the water, we left China further behind.

CHAPTER 28
THE FINAL ORCHESTRATION
DATELINE: NEW YORK CITY
(THAT SOUND OFFICIAL ENOUGH?)

"And this will be your office, Rusty," Sad said.

"What will I do in here?"

"You need an office. You will get…investigations to review."

"Investigations to investigate."

"To investigate. Yes."

There was a flat screen TV hanging off the wall with CNN playing. It really was a plush, big office.

"But first, there are a few more treatments that Dr. Suliman and I will administer."

"And drugs."

"And drugs, yes. You will have an assistant who will also be a driver for you."

"Where will I live? At a hotel?"

"For a while, yes. Until you think you want to stay somewhere else."

"Move…somewhere else?"

"Yes."

"Like a house or something?"

"Or something. Yes."

"So you will be watching over me for a while?"

"For a while."

There was a press conference starting on the TV screen. It was held outside a prison. Steverino Downing was being released this very afternoon. His wife and grown children were there. Lawyers. Peter was even there with the family. Downing walked up to a collection of microphones before the camera.

"I would like to thank the Freedom Foundation for making this happen," he said, nodding his head toward Peter. "For saving my life. I am told that the original detective on the case did some amazing work to set me free, too. Amazing. Risked his life to do it. I would like to thank Detective Rusty…"

"I am not a detective anymore," I said to the screen, shaking my head. Downing looked like he'd aged 20 years from the day I arrested him.

"Have you seen General Grant in a while?" she asked.

"No ma'am. He's abandoned me."

"You know, Downing has asked to see you. To thank you in person."

"Nope."

"Peter will bring them all straight here from this conference. We have services available for the people we free to help them adjust and settle back in…"

"…to this wonderful world we live in. I don't want to see him."

"He wants to thank you."

"I don't want him to thank me."

"Why?"

"I just don't. I didn't do this to be thanked. I did this because it was the right thing to do. That's all." Man! That flew right out of my mouth, like someone else said it. "You know, let him thank you, Sad. You orchestrated this whole soap opera."

"I think you will be just fine," Sad said, obviously thinking of my sudden, rah-rah, right-thing speech. "Some problems in this world are just bigger and faster than the civilized laws and courts can handle. We just need to be bigger and faster."

They watched the conference.

"Any local news out yet on the three missing NYPD detectives?" I asked while staring at the screen.

"None. Not a word," Sad said, while staring at the screen. "I don't know how they can hide that three officers are missing for weeks. Not even a public plea for help."

"And of course, nothing on two mobsters and the boat captain missing either," I summarized.

"Nothing."

"School shooting in China?"

"The local police and the local news say it was a Triad Gang shootout, and only gang members were shot and killed."

"The women in the school saw me."

"I wouldn't worry about it. I wouldn't go back to China for a while though."

A local DA talked on the TV next. Blather-blather-blah-blah.

"I need to go down to Agnes' house tomorrow. I left some stuff there."

"I will arrange that. You will have a car, and Lamont will drive you."

"Our office, in conjunction with the New York District Attorney's Office," the prosecutor continued, "and the FBI will be conducting an investigation into the facts of this case, even though the statute of limitations has expired on some of the felony charges."

"Good luck with all that," I said.

"Eventually they'll get around to interviewing you. I'll go with you as your counsel, which means you won't have to say a word. Talk to you later, Rusty," Sad said and left the room. She shut the door of…my office behind her.

I stared at my new TV. The office was all well and good, but we all know I am a dead man for sure. The Mob wants me dead. The Five Apes. The Shenyang Triad. Who knows how they feel about me in the Somali pirate gossip columns?

When the news conference ended, Peter escorted the family and the lawyer away from the podium. I stood in the center of the room. For a long while, actually. Stood there. "Bigger and faster," I remembered Sad said. Can I stay bigger and faster than all my enemies? All of my past.

Freeing Steverino was small and slow and not the end of this. This wasn't big enough and fast enough for me yet. I needed to get something from Agnes' back yard and then see a certain engraver I knew in Jersey City. One I trust. And then I needed to make one more business trip. By myself.

CHAPTER 29
BIGGEST. FASTEST.
BRATTLEBORO.
COLD LIKE LAST TIME.
SUNDAY NIGHT LIKE LAST TIME.

And Julian Managos was back in the bar watching football, like last time.

When the game was over, he left the bar, just like last time. He zipped up his short jacket, blew warm air into his fists and walked up the street. He was oblivious to me standing by the telephone pole and around some small trees near the sidewalk. Not at all far from where we first met about a month ago.

A few stores away, he looked up and saw me. He never even stutter-stepped, just kept his same pace. He shook his head at me.

"Tommy! Tommy from New York! Or should I say, the detective from New York," Julian said. His hands remained bundled inside his pockets; belly high.

"I've got a gun right on you. You pull your hands out, and I'll kill you."

He looked at the hand in the side pocket of my jacket, and he could see the print of my gun barrel pushing forward.

"So, the detective from New York. Detective Rusty."

"Once a detective. I'm not one anymore."

"They warned me about you. They said you were po-licing up your old messes. Said you freed that Downing guy from the pen. Saved his life from the needle. You're a little famous now, ain't cha?"

"You tell them we met?"

"No. No, I didn't want them to get any ideas."

"I understand. I understand. They tell you they are missing some of their men?"

"Nah."

"I guess they didn't want you getting any ideas," I said.

"How did you find me anyway?"

"The Cadillac."

He nodded. "Ahhh! Yeah. The caddy. Stupid, huh?"

"Not so stupid. Only I figured it out. No one else did."

"No one else cared," he said.

"When we met last time? I knew right away that you killed the China Doll," I told him. "You wrapped her up in a carpet. You hauled her up to Connecticut. You buried her there. You called Crime Stoppers. You framed an innocent man."

He shrugged and half-smiled. "That's a lot. A mouthful, detective. But, where's your evidence for a court of law? Seems to me you got nothing for a court a law."

"Court of law?" I looked at him dead in the eye. "Who said anything about a court of law?"

I shot that fucker right then and there. Bullet went through my coat pocket and into his chest. Then I pulled the gun out, racked the slide and extended my arm out straight. The pistol was a few feet from him. I shot him in the throat. I thought of the dead China Doll as I shot him. I saw her flash in my mind from the pictures in her house.

Julian fell back against a store front, hands on his throat, gurgling. He slipped down the wall. Something else slipped away. Pee stained his pants. His life slipped away.

"I'm not a detective anymore," I whispered at him. I let the pistol slip from my gloved hand. It clanged on the sidewalk. It was the pistol I took off of Detective Macelroy back at the Jersey shore clinic. Yeah, a plant. Now engraved.

It now had, "Detective Macelroy, N.Y.P.D." engraved on the side. Let the local police and newspapers figure out how a missing NYPD detective's pistol was found by a murdered, known, organized crime thug in Brattleboro, Vermont. A missing detective who is somehow not officially listed anywhere as missing. That was probably Macelroy's untraceable, "throw-down," gun, thus – the personalized engraving. It's hard for the newspapers to pass on the obvious engraving. That's news. Let them all sweat that out for a while.

I walked to my rental car and slipped inside. Some guys poured out of the bar down the corner, heads on swivels, looking around to see where the explosions came from. They couldn't see Julian's body from there. They couldn't even see me. I drove off, away from them. In the mirror, I saw them file back inside the bar. They didn't seem to care.

And, then I was gone. Gone. Today, I was the biggest and fastest.

IF YOU LIKE THIS, TAKE A LOOK AT:
BE BAD NOW BY HOCK HOCHHEIM

HOW BAD IS BAD ENOUGH WHEN YOU MUST...
BE BAD NOW?

In the 1980's a recession stampedes Texas. The oil industry dries up, laying high rollers low and sending the entire state of Texas into a tornado-like downspin. Northern mobsters invade these cracks in the Lone Star State. Their schemes: corruption, loan sharking, gambling, extortion, drug and human trafficking, and murder for hire -- all backed with strong arms swinging bats, psychos pointing guns, torture, violence and death.

The city of West Forge, a stone's throw from Houston, is Sgt. "Jumpin" Jack Kellog's town. When organized crime seeps in, Kellog's brand of justice knows no bounds. He tracks, fights, kicks and shoots his way through conspiracies, threats, ambushes and showdowns. Pushed to near-madness by angst with informants inside his agency and lurking everywhere, Jack tackles the thugs, bosses, lawyers, politicians and businessmen on the mob payroll, in a battle that takes him from the swamps of Louisiana, to the ghettos of Houston, to casinos in Vegas and even through the Halls of Congress in Washington D.C..

"If you like hard-core fast-moving police stories with a sense of justice, Be Bad Now is a definite read."

AVAILABLE NOW

ABOUT THE AUTHOR:

Hock Hochheim is a former U.S. Army investigator and 22 year veteran Texas police investigator, patrol officer, former private investigator and award winning author.

He currently owns and operates Force Necessary, an international combatives training company and teaches combat techniques and strategies in 11 allied countries around the world annually. He is the author of 10 non-fiction books and four fiction, and countless articles on policing, the military, street survival, close quarter combat and conflict psychology. He lives in Texas.

In 2013 Hock's book My Gun is My Passport won the Beverly Hills Book Award for Best Military Fiction. You may read more about him at http://www.forcenecessary.com or email him at hock@hockscqc.com